'I'm sorry abc

Drew was loung
evidently waiting for her to catch up
'You've had a soft life and now that things are
getting tough, you can't handle it!'

Christy's lips parted; Drew's words had been
flung at her with a casualness that stung.
'That's not true!' she flashed indignantly.

He raised a dark brow in query. 'Isn't it?'

Dear Reader

Summer might be drawing to an end—but don't despair!
This month's selection of exciting love stories is
guaranteed to bring back a little sunshine! Why not let
yourself be transported to the beauty of a Caribbean
paradise—or perhaps you'd prefer the exotic mystery of
Egypt? All in the company of a charming and
devastatingly handsome hero, naturally! Of course, you
don't have to go abroad to find true romance—and when
you're a Mills & Boon reader you don't even need to step
outside your front door! Just relax with this book, and
you'll see what we mean...

The Editor

Laura Martin lives in a small Gloucestershire village with
her husband, two young children and a lively sheepdog!
Laura has a great love of interior design and, together
with her husband, has recently completed the renovation
of their Victorian cottage. Her hobbies include
gardening, the theatre, music and reading, and she finds
great pleasure and inspiration from walking daily in the
beautiful countryside around her home.

SECRET SURRENDER

BY
LAURA MARTIN

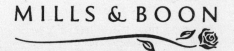

MILLS & BOON

MILLS & BOON LIMITED
ETON HOUSE, 18-24 PARADISE ROAD
RICHMOND, SURREY TW9 1SR

*MILLS & BOON and the Rose Device
are trademarks of the publisher.*

*First published in Great Britain 1994
by Mills & Boon Limited*

© Laura Martin 1994

*Australian copyright 1994   Philippine copyright 1994
This edition 1994*

ISBN 0 263 78625 0

*Set in Times Roman 10½ on 12 pt.
01-9409-52982 C*

Made and printed in Great Britain

CHAPTER ONE

'CHRISTY?' She could see him in the half-light, propped up on one elbow, watching her with a face that expressed incredulity and anger. 'Just where the hell do you think you're going?'

The hotel sheets didn't cover much of the powerful naked torso. Christy, in the second it took her to turn her head, appraised the glistening body with its sheen of sweat, found herself picturing the frantic activity that had gone on between them, on this most humid of summer nights. 'I . . . I thought you were asleep.' She continued her scramble in the grey light for her clothes. Her blouse had been retrieved but that wasn't enough—not if she wanted to escape the luxurious surroundings of this place without causing a riot.

'You haven't answered my question.' His voice was steel-edged, insistent, and Christy found herself trembling deep inside.

What on earth was she doing here? How had she ever allowed this to happen? She closed her eyes for a split-second and called herself all manner of names as she pulled her blouse frantically over her tousled, shiny blonde mane.

'Christy, come back to bed! It's past one in the morning.' It was a strong voice. Strong and deep and commanding. Used to being obeyed, used to having its wishes followed immediately, particularly when those wishes were directed at young, attractive females who barely had a stitch on.

But I'm not just another of his bimbos, Christy reminded herself desperately, frantically continuing her search for her clothes. I'm not! Her eyes were more used to the light now and she saw with relief a pile of clothing on the floor beside the bed. 'This is crazy! How did I ever get myself into this situation?' she whispered frantically. 'I...I've got to go; I should never have stayed—never!'

Since the ardour of their mutual passion had been extinguished so satisfactorily, that thought had been the only thing on her mind—that and what a fool she had made of herself. 'I've got to get out of here.' Her voice trembled noticeably as she cast her eyes towards the bed and with enormous effort she took a deep breath and added in stronger tones, 'I should never have come here. We should never have——'

Drew leant forward then and she felt the strength of his fingers curled around her upper arm, felt tingling deep in the pit of her stomach as the heat of his breath warmed the sensitive place between her neck and her shoulder-blade, sending shivers of desire down her spine, just like before. 'Christy, don't be so hasty.'

His voice had momentarily lost its edge, as if he too had fallen under the spell that had overwhelmed them so unexpectedly earlier in the evening. Her name sounded so sweet, so sensuous on his lips, beguiling her, trying to fool her all over again. And his mouth— oh, that was a sensation! How could kisses be so erotic, so tempting? Christy wondered, as her eyes began to close and her body momentarily swayed back against the strength of Drew Michaels' powerful chest.

'Don't be foolish,' he murmured huskily, running his mouth along the curve of her neck, sweeping her hair away with his large strong hands. 'You can't leave now. You know you can't.'

She was weakening all over again. Her resolve just seemed to melt away at the lightest of touches. She felt the sharp familiar ache of desire deep in the pit of her stomach and knew that time was running out; any more of this and she wouldn't be able to hold on, wouldn't be able to rescue what little pride and self-esteem she had left . . .

With a jerk Christy dragged herself free and stood up, stepping away from the bed, walking purposefully to the lamp over at the far side of the room. She clicked it on, steeling herself for the flood of light that would reveal Drew Michaels in all his glory, that would display the luxurious yet impersonal surroundings of the best suite in the hotel, and at the same time show up the extreme tackiness of the whole damnable situation that she had somehow allowed herself to slide into. She had always vowed that she would save herself for the right man . . . to be nearly twenty-three and still a virgin had been some kind of a record, she suspected—at least in the world she inhabited. But that was over now; she had thrown it all away in a moment of supreme stupidness.

He was angry. The sharp, tight angle of his jaw told her that, the ice in the steel-blue eyes. They had been like azure before, she thought distractedly, fresh, sparkling, like the colour of a perfect summer's sky. When he had smiled and dragged her into his arms for the first time, they had sparked with lust and sensuality.

What had been her undoing? Finally meeting him after all the hype and the expectation? Had that contributed in some way to what had followed? But why

should it have? she thought as she struggled into her
sleek linen skirt. She had met many famous people
before, many attractive men who were successful, who
commanded respect.

A tormented sigh escaped her lips. Who was she
kidding? None of them, not the powerful politicians,
nor the wealthy businessmen, nor the renowned auth-
orities on one subject or another, had possessed this
aura, this magnetism. All Drew Michaels had had to
do was stare long and hard with those magical deep
blue eyes as he murmured her name and held out his
hand in greeting and she was hooked—she along with
all the others . . .

Christy jerked her head up and saw that his mouth
was widening into the semblance of a smile now—a
cynical, mocking twist of the lips that held precious
little warmth, certainly no feeling. 'You're really intent
on leaving?' He lay back against the pillows, clasping
his hands behind his head, appraising Christy with a
look that chilled her through to the bone, because
suddenly he looked so cold and distant. 'And the night
is still so young! This is hardly the exit I would have
expected, Christy—a little undignified, don't you
think? Rather lacking in the composure that we've all
come to expect from so celebrated a television personality. What do you think the concierge will make
of your exit when you fling yourself out through the
main entrance at this time of the night?'

'If it's your reputation you're worried about——'
Christy began through tight lips.

'My reputation?' Drew let out a harsh laugh and
shook his head. 'Oh, no! Mine's past redemption, I'm
afraid, and besides, I've reached a stage in my life

where I'm past caring what other people think of me. Oh, no, Christy, it was actually yours I had in mind.'

Drew rose from the bed. His naked body was lean and taut, powerful, thrilling with its mat of dark hair covering the sculptured chest, the strong solidness of his thighs, his abdomen . . .

'Take a look in the mirror, Christy—see how beautiful you look: tousled, fulfilled . . . Do it!' Drew placed commanding hands on her waist, twisted her around so that he was standing behind her, so that she had no choice but to do as he bid. 'Go on—take a look at yourself.'

She swallowed, fighting hard against the instinct to hold her head in her hands as she viewed their reflection in the full-length mirror. It was a striking combination: two physically attuned bodies, tall, athletic figures with features that were in stark contrast. Drew rugged and darkly handsome, with hair as black as night. Christy lithe and elegant with a delicate face, a halo of golden hair.

Drew spanned his hands against her stomach, pulling the fabric of her silk blouse taut so that the outline of her full breasts was clearly visible beneath. She watched and felt the stirring of desire, saw the evidence of her own weakness as their outline became more and more prominent. 'You see how good we look together, Christy? How easily your body registers its need? Once is never enough; let me make love to you again, let me fulfil your desires again and again . . .'

Her breathing was rapid now, as if oxygen was at a premium. Drew's gaze, his voice dripped sexuality, contributing as much to the way she felt as the thrill of his hands on the smooth, flat plane of her stomach.

She hated herself for this weakness. It shocked her that despite everything she could still be tempted to turn and press herself against the sculptured body, to lift her face and accept the ravaging hunger of his mouth. It had felt like pure heaven before, in that moment when desire had overtaken sense, in that length of time that had felt like eternity and no time at all, and despite everything the need to experience such a pinnacle of pleasure again and again was strong within.

'No!' Somehow, from somewhere, she dragged up enough resistance. It had been a fool's paradise, she knew that, didn't she? Hadn't she experienced dreadful despair as soon as that most glorious sensation had been reached because she had allowed Drew to make love to her purely for physical reasons alone? 'No!' Christy ran a shaky hand through her hair and then jerked herself free. 'I'm leaving, Drew and I'm leaving now!' She turned, struggling for a moment to keep hold of what little composure she had left, then she spun back around to face him, to stare Drew in the eyes and make him believe that what she was about to say was the truth. 'Can't you understand that I feel dreadful, like a stranger inside? I've allowed this to happen. I've allowed a man I don't know, don't particularly like even, to make love to me...' Her voice trailed miserably away—even now she could hardly believe that she had allowed herself to be seduced.

'You make it sound as if you were an unwilling participant,' Drew murmured with a casual quietness that seemed only to emphasise the ice beneath his words, 'when in fact we both know that you were feverish, passionate—dare I say desperate?—to secure a union between us.'

He stunned her with his cruel bluntness for all of three slow seconds. 'My God, I hate you!' Christy's violet eyes blazed with dislike. 'I must have been mad ... or drunk ... or ...'

'You were neither and you know it!' Drew growled menacingly. 'As soon as we laid eyes on one another we both knew the outcome of this evening. We made love because it was what we both wanted and don't you dare start pretending otherwise!'

'Don't you presume to tell me how to behave!' Christy snapped, swinging back round to face him. 'I'll act just however I feel like acting! Don't think you can talk to me like all the other women you entice into your bed. I lost my senses for a couple of hours, but they're back now and in full working order.'

'Are they?' Drew raised a dark enquiring brow and something in his expression, some hint of what was to come perhaps, sent a shiver of trepidation down Christy's spine. 'This is hardly as your public usually sees you, is it? Composed and in control at all times, isn't that the Christy King maxim? "The ice-cool goddess of the small screen"—wasn't that how one columnist recently described you? So what happens when we meet tomorrow? When we face one another in the studio? How cool will the icy interviewer Miss King be then, I wonder?'

That had been his parting shot, and the next day in the studio he had proceeded to make life as difficult as possible for her...

'I believe I'm particularly honoured this evening; you don't give interviews as a rule, do you, Mr Michaels?' Christy managed somehow to force her widest, most appealing smile, purely for the viewers' benefit, of course, and waited with bated breath for his answer. A direct, no-nonsense first question. Why should she change her tactics? she thought.

He took his time, oblivious, it seemed, of the fact that several million viewers were waiting on his reply. Were nerves a part of this man's make-up? Christy wondered, as she registered her own familiar thudding heart and damp palms.

'Interviews are a rather boring and incredibly ego-tistical way of passing the time,' he drawled, leaning one arm along the back of his chair. 'To be honest—and of course I realise that that is what you of all people would want, Christy,' he added with more than a hint of sarcasm, his mouth widening into a charming, all too attractive smile that no doubt sent millions of Michaels fans swooning over their tele-vision sets, 'I can think of a hundred and one things I would rather be doing at this very moment.'

'Such as?' Christy asked swiftly, leaning forward slightly in her chair, determined not to let this un-promising start get the better of her. 'What would you be doing now, Mr Michaels, if you weren't sitting here talking to me?' She raised questioning eyebrows and tried to look as if she really wanted to know, as if she cared about the answer.

Drew's mouth twisted suggestively, his eyes nar-rowed, and for several calculating seconds he stayed silent. What was he going to say? Christy felt the automatic shiver race through her body as sexual tension sparked between them. She tried not to think about the night before and failed dreadfully. 'I think perhaps I'd better leave that to the imagination,' he murmured after a moment. 'Suffice to say it would involve soft lights, wine and a very attractive female.'

The audience laughed at the deliberate heavy sexual innuendo he had put into his reply and Christy, much to her chagrin, blushed; she just couldn't do a thing about it. The audience didn't know, of course; no one knew that she of all people had allowed Drew to make love to her, that she had been seduced so very easily in exactly that way, but that knowledge didn't stop her feeling heart-stoppingly anxious. How can he be doing this to me? she thought wildly. What shall I say now? What shall I do? I want to get out of here, she screamed silently, listening to the noise in her earpiece from the gallery above where the director and his assistants sat. How many minutes left? How many?

'But duty calls,' Drew continued with a dismissive shrug. 'I decided that I would plunge into the rather disagreeable depths of promotion for the benefit of my latest project and so here I am—completely at your mercy.'

Who are you kidding? Christy thought angrily, watching the relaxed features, the twist of a smile. 'Er... you put up a great deal of your own money for this film, I believe?' she continued with determined briskness.

'Almost all.'

'You must have a lot of faith in its potential. What made you take such a risk? After all there is a recession on; this is not supposed to be the best of times for launching new ideas.'

'On the contrary,' he responded crisply, 'good things rise to the top no matter what the economic climate; indifferent and average commodities sink without a trace, and as far as I am concerned that is how it should be.'

'The script must be very good.'

His eyes were glacial, there was an expression of bored disdain written clearly on the smooth, tanned face. 'Yes. I wrote it myself!'

Christy shifted slightly in her seat, her fingers curling tensely around the arms of her swivel chair, her bright expression fixed hopelessly, and waited, knowing that his reply was over, but waiting just the same. 'Perhaps you'd care to tell us a little about the film?' Her voice was still light, still sounded remarkably relaxed, despite the painful tension within. Would he continue with this almost monosyllabic massacre to the very end? Would he really make it that hard?

'This film is what people wish to make of it. Funny in parts, dramatic, thrilling, tense, sad——'

'Sounds too good to be true!' Christy cut in lightly. 'Surely it's not possible to introduce so many elements in one piece of drama?'

He raised dark eyebrows and threw her a casual look. 'Really? And why not?' he enquired composedly. 'Do you know something that I don't about the film business, Miss King?'

She floundered like a fish out of water as he waited with deliberate cool for *her* to answer *his* question. 'Well...I...' She hesitated and cursed herself for falling into the trap of asking a question that hadn't been thought through, that hadn't been planned. He had unsettled her and she had said the first thing that had come into her head. 'Well...' Why couldn't she think quickly enough? 'Er...films tend to fall into categories, don't they? I——'

'Films as in life—there are many elements, Miss King.'

Silence.

She wanted to throttle him. To get up out of her chair and wipe that superior, slightly amused expression from his face. I could at least get up and walk away, she thought. What's stopping me?

'I believe you were once quoted as saying that you despised money? Rather a weird statement from someone who's as wealthy as you, surely?' Pick the bones out of this one, Michaels! Christy thought, relieved that she had changed tack so quickly. 'After all, we read at very frequent intervals various things about your extravagant lifestyle——'

'And you believe it all?' He gave a small shake of his head and produced a brilliant, totally relaxed smile, gazing with stunning eyes at Christy, managing to produce just the right effect: a mixture of disbelief and genuine amusement, coupled with the implication that perhaps Christy was more than just a little bit dim.

'So exactly what do you do with your millions, Mr Michaels?' she enquired with ill-concealed annoyance. 'Surely you aren't trying to tell us you live like a monk?'

'Not at all—anyone who believes that would have to be very foolish.'

Christy gripped the leather arm-rest and tried not to allow the cutting reply to get to her. 'So you do indulge in extravagant luxuries, then?'

'You seem rather obsessed by other people's wealth, Miss King. Why is that?'

'Obsessed? No...I'm——'

'Aren't I right in saying,' Drew continued, 'that you're the highest paid female on television?'

'Oh, no——'

'You're telling me that's not a fact?'

His perfectly timed question was delivered with the utmost precision—any other time and Christy would have almost admired it. 'Well—er——' Stop stuttering, you fool! she told herself angrily. Say something. He's getting the better of you! 'I admit to earning a substantial amount,' she conceded finally, forcing a smile that masked, she hoped, all of her awkwardness and her animosity. 'But I'm sure the viewers don't want to know about me——'

'Oh, no false modesty, Christy, please,' Drew delivered smoothly. 'Credit your audience with more intelligence. How do you like to spend your wealth, Miss King? Or do you give it all away?'

'Look——' There was no mistaking her own annoyance now. She heard the audience collectively snigger and in that moment knew that she had failed miserably. 'If we could just get back to you, I'm sure——'

'You're not doing as well as I had hoped,' Drew remarked casually, 'and I have to confess a certain amount of disappointment. I was led to believe you were one of the best when it came to interviewing, Miss King.'

Christy gulped back her shock and struggled to come up with some sort of half-decent reply. 'I...I find that you're rather a difficult personality to get to grips with, Mr Michaels,' she retorted swiftly.

A smile tugged the corners of his mouth. 'That's not what you said last night!' he drawled casually.

Christy paled visibly beneath the bright lights as the audience chuckled again. A joke, they imagined—if only, Christy thought desperately, if only...

And so it went on...and on...and on...

* * *

She had been a fool to imagine for one moment that she could handle him, of course, that he wouldn't reap his revenge in some sort of sadistic way. Seven million people had witnessed her verbal humiliation on live television and to this day she still hadn't truly managed to get over it.

'Christy?' She jumped a mile and glanced across to the door. 'I did knock.' Lizzie smiled and then a frown of concern furrowed her brow. 'You OK? You look a bit peaky. Not sickening for something, I hope.'

'No, no!' Christy hastily pulled herself together and picked up a comb. 'You just startled me a little, that was all.' She managed a watery smile. 'I was miles away.'

'Planning all the wonderful things you're going to do after this evening?'

Stop thinking about him. Stop it! Christy took a deep breath and made an effort to stay with the present. Three years ago, she told herself angrily; stop going over it!

She took a huge breath and determinedly thrust away the images that insisted on haunting her. 'Umm ... sorry, what did you say, Lizzie?'

Her friend's grey eyes widened teasingly. 'Hey, you really are in a daydream, aren't you? I know this is the last one in the series, but you still have tonight's show to do, you know!'

Christy managed a vague smile. 'Lizzie ...' she frowned slightly and then made her voice sound casual '... that scent you're wearing. I noticed it when you came in before—it's new, isn't it?'

Lizzie raised her hand and smelled the inside of her wrist before offering the same to Christy. 'Mmm, I like it. But it's not perfume; I borrowed some of Paul's incredibly expensive aftershave this morning, I was in such a hurry to get out of the house...'

That was what had started it. So distinctive, not powerful, nor overwhelming, but invasive. Drew had been wearing it that night; the smell had become a part of her as their bodies had entwined together...

'Time I was out of here,' Christy murmured, glancing at her wristwatch. 'Five minutes before transmission. I'll see you after the show, OK?'

CHAPTER TWO

'AND that, I'm afraid, is just about it for this series. I'd like to thank my guests this evening—the Right Honourable...'

Christy's mouth smiled effortlessly as she delivered her closing lines into the television camera, her startling violet-blue eyes skimming the autocue with practised ease. One final heart-stopping curve of her scarlet lips, a slight pause and then her husky, 'Goodnight,' and she was swivelling casually back in her by now famous leather chair to chat to her guests as the studio lights dimmed and the credits rolled and the audience clapped their usual enthusiastic response.

She heard the voice of Jeff, the director, in the radio earpiece she wore, telling her that they were off air and that she had just completed yet another great hour of live television, and with an inward sigh of relief she stood up, smiling, to shake hands once again with her guests who had spent the last hour discussing themselves and revealing their innermost thoughts with the viewing nation.

A quick smile and a wave to the studio audience, and then she was disappearing around the back of the elegant set and along the maze of corridors that lead to her dressing-room.

'How did it go?' Lizzie, lounging comfortably in one of the two armchairs with a sheaf of papers, looked up and pulled a face. 'Was it that bad?'

19

'Are you kidding?' Christy flopped down into the other and stretched her slim golden arms far above her head. 'I thought that final thirty minutes was never going to end. Did you see it on the set in here? That last old fool hardly let me get a word in edgeways!'

'Better than having someone who clams up completely like earlier this month,' Lizzie reminded her lightly. 'You were nearly at your wits' end then, remember?'

Christy shook her head and gave a tired smile. 'Don't remind me! The only trouble was tonight's guest didn't say a thing that was worth listening to! I told them I had doubts about him as a guest, but as usual nobody took any notice.'

She rose from the chair in one graceful movement and crossed to the brightly lit dressing-table, slipping off her elegantly styled flame-coloured dress. 'Still, why am I complaining? It's over, another series completed.' She turned, pausing in her task of removing the heavy make-up that was needed for the television cameras, as glamorous and beautiful as any highly paid model with her tumbling blonde hair and perfectly formed features, and produced a smile that shone.

She had been a fool to allow the old stupid memories to intrude, especially tonight of all nights. She had been looking forward to this moment for days, weeks. 'Well, I'm free, Lizzie! I'm free!'

'Not exactly free,' her friend reminded her seriously. 'You're straight into the work for this new series of radio interviews; you haven't forgotten, have you?'

'Don't look so worried! Of course I haven't forgotten,' Christy replied lightly. 'I meant I'm free from the restrictions of working three nights a week in this hell-hole.' She threw back her head and began to brush vigorously at her hair until it shone. 'God, how I'm sick of the routine.' She paused, hairbrush in hand, and glanced across at Lizzie, her large violet eyes instantly assessing her friend's thoughts. 'Now don't look at me like that. I know you think I'm an ungrateful devil, Lizzie—that there are a hundred thousand women out there who would give their eye-teeth to do what I do, but any job becomes boring if you do it long enough and you must admit I've done more shows here than I can remember.'

'And what's wrong with that?' Lizzie asked, in her usual earnest manner. 'You're outstanding at what you do, Christy. The ratings keep on going up, they offer you more money each time your contract is due for renewal just to make sure you stay—what more do you want for goodness' sakes?'

Christy breathed a sigh and gazed at her reflection in thoughtful contemplation. How could she explain? A great chunk of her felt guilty for even thinking about wanting more. It wasn't wealth—Lizzie was right, the company did keep throwing money at her just so that she would stay. Goodness knew she earned more now than she knew what to do with. Such a mind-blowing contrast from the hateful years at the children's home, when personal possessions had been practically non-existent, and bright, glamorous futures, such as the one Christy had found, had been merely dreams.

She released a sigh, thrusting away the old images that still had the ability to depress her a little if she dwelt too long on them. 'Life's good, Lizzie, I know that. I've come a long way—further than I ever would have dreamed,' Christy replied with unusual urgency, 'but there are still things to do, avenues to explore . . .' She paused, frowning as she tried to form her thoughts and feelings into satisfactory sentences, ones that would enable her friend to understand. 'I want . . . well, I suppose personal satisfaction describes it best. An inner contentment.' She shook her head and smiled self-consciously. 'Listen to me! Don't I sound serious? Oh, take no notice, Lizzie, I've had one of those days; I just need a change, that's all.' She pulled a comical grimace in the mirror at her own reflection. 'I know you think I'm mad——'

'Well, I didn't say that exactly——' Lizzie replied hastily.

Christy smiled teasingly. 'Now don't bother trying to hide that expression; it's too late.' She turned back to the mirror and added moisturiser to her smooth face with a careful sweep of her fingers. 'Perhaps it's just ambition burning through me, like one of those joke candles that refuses to be extinguished. Only on my particular cake,' Christy smiled, 'there isn't just one, there's a whole blazing inferno driving me on, pushing me relentlessly forward. Anyway,' she added with determined brightness, vowing silently that she must stop indulging in this dreadful self-analysis, 'let's look ahead. Have you got the rest of the information on the King series?'

Lizzie delved into her large briefcase and rummaged around for a few seconds before handing over some papers. 'That's the confirmed list of interviewees,' she explained. 'Eight in total, from every walk of life imaginable. Everything's been arranged. All you have to do is get to work on your questions and then record.'

Christy's long slim fingers flicked through the papers, her eyes skimming over the details, most of which were known to her already. The whole idea for a series of radio interviews set in the subject's own chosen surroundings had been her idea in the first place. 'Mmm, looks fine. They've stuck with most of my suggestions too. Good.' She lifted her head and gave a satisfied nod.

'Er... I believe they had trouble with a couple of choices and I don't know if you noticed but at the end there—er—they added one.'

'Oh?' Christy bent her head once again, her hair falling like a curtain around her face as she scanned the list, vaguely intrigued because suddenly Lizzie sounded hesitant, and that wasn't like her at all.

'Oh, no!' Her tone was softly incredulous, totally disbelieving. She flung back her head in an angry movement and then reread that certain name that always, always made her blood boil. 'Lizzie, why is this man's name here?' she demanded in shaky tones. 'Is... is this some kind of joke?' She leant forward and stabbed at the paper with a long shiny red fingernail. 'Look, here!'

She knew it wasn't. Lizzie would never do such a thing to her. She didn't know about... Christy swiftly averted her thoughts... but she knew how much she detested the man, didn't she? 'Lizzie, there is no way in the world I am interviewing him ever again—not after last time, not after the way he treated me! How long have you known?' She pushed back the swivel chair and paced the room, almost frantically, her thoughts whirring. 'Well, it's impossible! Absolutely out of the question, totally out of the question!'

It was quite a sight—Christy King in full, ferocious
action. She stormed up and down the dressing-room,
glaring at Lizzie, at the paper that dared to so much
as print his name, and then at her reflection in the
wall of mirrors.

'You've signed,' Lizzie reminded matter-of-factly,
unperturbed by her friend's hot temper. 'There's not
a lot you can do about it——'

'Oh, can't I?' Christy grabbed at her change of
clothing from its hanger and swiftly pulled on the elegant grey trouser suit. 'Well, we'll see about that!'
She picked up her large leather holdall and stuffed
the papers angrily into one of the compartments. 'No
one forces me to interview that man again—no one!'
She marched to the door of her dressing-room and
wrenched it open. 'Oh, Lizzie!' She paused, turning
back with a look that conveyed all her anguish. Part
of her wanted to tell. To unburden everything on to
the shoulder of a friend, especially one as close as
Lizzie, was suddenly tempting in the extreme. But
confidences, especially ones so personal, didn't come
naturally. Too many childhood years of locking up
emotions, of having to rely on her own resources to
see her through had caused that. 'Please understand
it's not that I'm angry with you or anything...but
you...you see...it's not just because of that awful
interview I did with him all those years ago...' She
hesitated, biting at her bottom lip for a moment and
then shook her head. 'No...no, don't worry. It doesn't
matter. I'll say goodnight, Lizzie; I've got to go and
sort this thing out. I'll call you in the morning.'

Usually she paused at the entrance gate of the television studios and signed the pieces of paper that were
thrust through the window of her long, sleek Jaguar.

It was perhaps one of the reasons she was so popular. Always, always she took time to stop and chat a little to the regulars who gathered there to see her after the show. Driving past as if she were far too important, the way many a celebrity was inclined to do, never occurred to her. This evening was totally different, though. She whizzed through the gate at breakneck speed without so much as a glance in the direction of the loyal cluster of admirers.

His name, continually buzzing around and around in her head, was driving her mad. What was going on? she wondered desperately, as she roared off through the London traffic towards her home. Drew Michaels hated being photographed, let alone interviewed, so how on earth had his name landed at the bottom of the extremely exclusive list of interviewees?

Christy glared through the windscreen, drumming her fingers impatiently on the steering-wheel as she brought her Jaguar to a halt at a red light, and tried not to think about the possibility that she might *have* to interview the most audacious, most arrogant man who surely had ever walked on the surface of the planet again, whether she liked it or not.

It was a thought that was too awful to contemplate.

The car in front was slow pulling away and as the lights turned green Christy pressed her hand down on the horn and blasted for all she was worth. It didn't make her feel a great deal better, but it helped.

'What do you mean, *he offered* to be interviewed? Drew Michaels hates being interviewed! He would never do a thing like that.' Christy listened impatiently as the calming voice on the other end of the telephone line tried to explain something that would

never be to her satisfaction. 'So, because he's a big
star, because it's too good a chance to pass by, I'm
going to have to go along with all this—is that what
you're saying?' she continued in icy tones. 'Well, I'm
not so sure I want to be involved any more.' Christy
took a calming breath that did little to make her feel
any better, and continued with just the same amount
of anger, her voice rising with every syllable. 'And
this whole series was my idea; doesn't that count for
anything, don't I have the slightest say? Yes, yes, I
know I've signed . . .' She listened some more. Her
spirits were sinking fast. Drew Michaels, former actor
turned best-selling novelist, meant a lot. He was a
catch. Three years since that fateful interview and he
hadn't done another one since. Oh, yes, she thought
despondently, you may be the darling of the chat-show
hosts, Christy King, but you're in the minor league
when it comes to the likes of Mr Drew Michaels. You
or him and they'd drop you like a shot! She knew
only too well that there were a good handful of well-
established TV personalities just waiting to leap into
her shoes at the first opportunity.

Christy put down the phone with a resounding click
after hearing a few more placatory sentences, and lay
back against the pillows to stare up at the ruched silk
canopy over her bed. She was mad. Anger surged
through her veins like molten lava. Had Drew
Michaels set this whole thing up deliberately? It would
suit his perverted kind of thinking perfectly.

Oh, but that was ridiculous! Why on earth would
he care? She had just been another in a long line of
women; she knew that much only too well. Hardly a
week went by without some snippet of gossip reaching
the tabloid press and, even if fifty per cent of the sal-

acious stories about Drew and his numerous liaisons were untrue, as any intelligent person would surmise, that still left the other fifty per cent.

With a despondent sigh, Christy rose from her elegant four-poster bed and walked through to the *en suite* bathroom frantically trying to decide what to do.

Christy generously tipped the taxi driver and wondered why she hadn't cancelled her dinner arrangement with Conrad. She wasn't in any kind of mood for social chit-chat or even long companionable silences, which was what the two of them had seemed to indulge in recently.

She sighed and adjusted her long, sleek skirt. Still, here she was and she might as well make the best of it—after all, it wasn't Conrad's fault that Drew Michaels had somehow managed to intrude into her life again after all these years of carefully blotting him from her memory.

Making an entrance came naturally. It wasn't contrived or planned, it just seemed to happen. Being almost six feet tall helped, of course. Possessing a cascade of waist-length golden hair helped a little too, and add to that a face and a figure that automatically made heads turn, and a flair and style that was second to none, and Christy just couldn't help but be noticed.

She glided through the restaurant's hustle and bustle, making her way purposefully to her favourite table at the back of the room—perfectly placed so as to see and yet not be seen. It was *her* table—that was how she always thought of it. And why not? she thought now. She had patronised this place for years, right back to the early days of her career.

She glanced at her watch and predicted that Conrad would by now have her usual Martini waiting for her on the table, would be scanning the wine list with his usual care.

The place was certainly busy tonight. There was a buzz of lively conversation that almost drowned out the jazz pianist in the far corner. Christy spotted a few faces she knew and smiled her acknowledgement, before heading over to the far corner of the room where her table nestled behind a Japanese-style screen.

'Hi, Conrad. Sorry I'm a little late. Have you order——' She was almost sitting down in her usual seat before Christy realised that she wasn't talking to Conrad, but to a young stylish redhead with a cleavage like a mountain pass. 'Oh!' Christy's mouth formed the exclamation for a brief moment as she digested the fact that someone else was sitting at her table. She recovered in a fraction of a second and gave an apologetic smile. 'I'm afraid there must be some mistake——'

'It's OK, Christy, we're in a forgiving mood.'

It was a magnetically deep voice, a curious mixture of the accents from both sides of the Atlantic. Several years ago it had given countless numbers of film-goers reason to laugh and weep in their cinema seats, had attracted an adoring female following.

It was practically unmistakable.

With a fierce jerk of her head, and an almost painful jolt of her heart, Christy's eyes swivelled sharply to the other side of the table, narrowing with incredulity as she focused on the compelling features of Drew Michaels. She took a sharp intake of breath, pursing her lips angrily as his generous mouth widened into a heart-stopping, but altogether infuriating, attractive smile.

'Care to join us, Miss King?' The stunning sapphire eyes mirrored his amusement. He raised one enquiring brow and stared at Christy through dark, spiky lashes. 'Well, well!' he drawled after three or four slow seconds of silence in which Christy could do nothing except stare. 'A celebrated chat-show host lost for words? I find that very hard to believe.'

His gaze travelled the length of her, surveying the halter-style top and matching long plum skirt, with its fashionable sexy thigh-length split, as if he had all the time in the world. As if, Christy thought angrily, she were a possible acquisition that needed one last look before purchase.

'This is *my* table,' Christy ground out through clenched teeth, aware that Drew Michaels had become, if that were possible, even more devastatingly attractive since she had last laid eyes on him.

Dark thick hair, left a little long. Piercing eyes that seemed somehow to delve right into her very soul... Christy took a breath and shifted her gaze from his face. He was dressed in his usual, understated mode: dark jacket, white shirt that was undone casually at the neck, revealing just a hint of strong dark hair, just a hint that the body beneath was tanned and bronzed, full of power and potent male strength. He was so...so blatantly masculine, she thought, forcing herself to think impersonally about him. He exuded an unexplainable aura of self-confidence, of personal relaxation. Nothing seemed to faze him at all. Nothing. But then that was because he didn't give a damn.

'This is your table? Indeed?' His lips twitched with sarcastic amusement. 'And there was I with the im-

pression that the restaurant owned everything.' He
raised an enquiring brow. 'Or are you a shareholder?
Does the Christy King empire extend to this most exclusive of eating houses now?'

'You know what I mean!' Christy replied with crisp
acidity, struggling to appear calm, despite everything,
despite the fact that she was suddenly seething like a
raving-mad woman underneath her glossy exterior. 'I
booked this table two days ago.' Assuming this aloof,
almost haughty expression was practically killing her.
She took another deep breath when it was clear he
wasn't going to answer and raised herself up to her
full height. 'I *always* sit here,' she added tightly. There
was pomposity in her tone and she regretted it immediately. For some reason only *this* man could do
this to her, she thought angrily—bring out the worst
part of her nature at a moment's notice.

'But not, it seems, tonight.' Drew Michaels threw
her a bored smile and leant back against his chair,
picking up the menu as he did so, scanning it casually
as if the subject were closed, dismissing Christy as if
she were no more than a waitress come to the table
with the wrong order.

'Just who the hell do you think you are?' Christy
grated, losing a little of her hard-fought-for composure. 'I suppose you just waltzed in here and sat
down in the first place that took your eye!'

Drew raised his head and cast Christy another distinctly bored glance. 'No. As a matter of fact we were
shown here by Roland, the owner himself. He told us
this was the best table in the house, didn't he,
Annette?' Drew smiled fondly across at his companion, who, Christy noticed, was looking slightly
bemused and embarrassed, 'and wished us a pleasant

evening. Of course at that stage,' he added with deliberate, cutting sarcasm, 'he wasn't to know we were going to be verbally accosted by a deranged chat-show hostess.'

'How dare you?' Christy's tone was as sharp as the look in her eyes. 'I could sue you for slander, or for defamation of character, or...or whatever the proper term is.'

'And I could call Roland to settle the argument and take great pleasure in making you look very small!' Drew informed her with quiet menace. 'Do yourself a favour, Miss King: retreat now, while you still have some shred of credibility left.'

'Christy!'

She turned, breathless with annoyance, to find Conrad at her elbow, to find practically the whole restaurant listening with avid attention, their eyes swivelled as one in the direction of her, Drew, and the desirable table she was laying claim to.

A long, slow, very, very hot flush rose steadily from the base of her neck up to her face, covering every inch of visible flesh in a vivid puce. So long since she had blushed, so long since she had found herself at the wrong end of a foolish situation. The last time had been three years ago, hadn't it? With this same, impossible man.

What on earth *was* she doing? She flinched inwardly and wished the ground would open up and swallow her.

Christy swivelled her head sharply back around and found herself looking at a highly amused Drew Michaels.

'Christy, we're sitting somewhere else,' Conrad whispered, putting himself between her and the other interested diners. 'Roland apologised but hoped we'd understand as it's just for this evening. You don't mind, do you?' Conrad's voice was low, embarrassed. He always hated any kind of a scene, Christy thought bitterly, always so well-mannered, so proper, so damn meek! 'It's over here,' he continued hurriedly; 'quite nice, by the window. I've ordered your Martini.'

'There, Miss King, a quite nice table by the window. All sorted!' He was mocking Conrad. Such a contrast between the two of them, she realised, such a difference... 'Now, there's no need to apologise for making such a fuss,' Drew added smoothly. 'It's just gratifying to know that you're capable of making mistakes like the rest of us mere mortals.'

'Very funny!' Christy snapped, putting every ounce of cold dislike she could into her gaze, while frantically scanning her brain for some last parting shot, some witty put-down that would help her out of this mess.

It was happening again. Why? Why did her brain always go like stodgy rice pudding when it mattered most—when Drew Michaels was around?

'Christy!' Conrad placed a light hand coaxingly on her bare back.

She didn't move. There were three choices, she decided swiftly. Stay and argue further and look even more ridiculous, go and sit with Conrad and practically choke trying to eat a meal, knowing the whole of the place was gossiping about her, or walk out with head held high and refuse ever to eat in this place again.

Her mind instinctively ran over the last time she had had occasion to meet 'God's gift—first to the silver screen and now to the literary world'. The party had been one of the best: well-planned, sumptuous. Full of famous faces. His had been the most famous, of course, an unexpected arrival that had had Vicki, the host, in raptures.

A thoughtful expression spread over Christy's face as she remembered that night. It had been an enjoyable moment, cutting him completely dead, spearing him with a look of icy aloofness in front of at least a dozen people. He had continued to smile that slow, lazy smile of his, thrown her a look of amusement that had been a little galling at the time, but underneath it all she had just known he was seething. Oh, yes, maybe it had been a small revenge for the way he had treated her, but it had been a sweet one nevertheless.

But it wasn't enough. And here, *here* was another occasion. If she didn't take her chance now, she would never get another opportunity—unless... Christy considered swiftly, running through the newly occurred possibility that maybe, just maybe, if she played her hand very carefully, she could turn everything around.

Three years on. There was just no comparison between the promising young model turned hopeful chat-show host and the sharp, respected interviewer she was today. And she was ready for him this time. Drew Michaels, she thought, aware of her own sudden quickening heart, could surely, with careful questioning, be made to look foolish at the very least.

'Unless you would both care to join us? Foursomes aren't generally my thing, but in the circumstances I'm willing to make an exception.'

Christy's gaze fell to a glass of wine, placed temptingly near to her hand. To throw the contents full in his face appealed to her enormously. Childish, of course, quite out of keeping with her character, but oh, how pleasurable to take that smug look off his face, to still the mobile mouth and dancing eyes for just a moment.

But then, weren't there far better ways to get her own back, to even the score? Damn it! Why should she allow him to dominate her life? That time, three years ago, needed laying to rest; she needed to settle the score.

She would interview him.

Out of the corner of her eye she saw Conrad turn back, hesitate, look pleased about the invitation to join Drew. After all, it was an opportunity not to be missed. He would probably never have the chance of dinner with one of the world's highest paid, most powerful and most famous men again, and she knew, much to her annoyance, that Conrad was a great fan of the man himself.

Drew pulled out a chair and gestured to it with a deliberate theatrical sweep of his arm. Playing to the crowd, that was what he was doing, making the most of her discomfort, milking the scene for all it was worth—just like last time.

That clinched it.

'I'll see you in a week's time, Michaels, but for now—drop dead!' Christy hissed, and with a haughty flick of her head and a flounce of her skirts she left Conrad standing alone and vacated the premises with a sharp click of her heels.

CHAPTER THREE

CHRISTY frowned irritably and cast narrowed eyes over the vast array of appealing clothes that were housed in her magnificent walk-in wardrobe. Usually she had no problem—no problem at all. But what to wear? What to pack for these damned two days with Drew Michaels—for a weekend that promised to be living purgatory and hell all rolled into one?

He had been irritatingly reticent about the situation of his newest home; secret hide-aways were his speciality—he had a retreat in almost every continent and the exact whereabouts of each one was a well-guarded secret.

Still, Christy decided, determined to be positive, determined not to let self-doubt and fear of what lay ahead eat away at her self-confidence, at her resolution to go through with this no matter what, it was only for two days and it was summer, and she would hardly be roughing it. Drew Michaels was renowned for his good taste in all things. Wherever she would be spending this hateful weekend, it was sure to be in the height of luxury.

The week since the incident in the restaurant had passed all too quickly and as Christy waited with nervous impatience for the car that would take her to his abode she found that not one ounce of annoyance had subsided in that far too short a time. Anger burned away inside, niggling her day and night like an ant bite that simply got redder and more painful.

The sudden blast of a car horn just then made her jump a mile. Silently cursing the driver for disturbing the discreet, tasteful ambience of this most exclusive of neighbourhoods, Christy peered cautiously around one of the ruched lace blinds in her drawing-room and glared at the shiny red Ferrari with scowling irritation. Typical, she thought, that he should employ someone with about the same amount of good manners as himself!

'Haven't you heard of doorbells?' Christy enquired, lowering her head to the open car-door window. 'Residents around here don't appreciate a blast of a car horn at nine o'clock on a Saturday morning! Oh!' She paused and straightened up as Drew Michaels opened the driver's door and appeared, looking disgustingly fit and healthy. 'It's you.'

'In the flesh.' He cast her a glance, surveying Christy with a critical eye, and immediately the prickles of antagonism that seemed to spring so easily to the surface whenever she set eyes on him were in action.

'Something the matter?' Her voice held enough ice to cause frostbite as she glanced swiftly down at her own attire and picked off a minuscule piece of fluff that was adhering to the finely cut cream trousers she had elected to wear.

Drew shrugged broad shoulders and shook his head with a smile that left Christy feeling a little too uncomfortable. 'No, not at all. I was just thinking how good, if not altogether practical, you were looking.' He came around and removed the portable radio equipment and the well-filled holdall from Christy's reluctant grasp—giving anything at all to Drew Michaels went against the grain. 'Forget anything?'

he asked pointedly, glancing down at the bulging leather. 'After all, you are going to be away from home for all of one night!'

Christy threw him a withering look. 'I happen to take a pride in my appearance—unlike some,' she added pointedly, casting derisive eyes over his attire of faded denims, battered trainers and a well-worn shirt, which was wound up at the elbows to reveal solid biceps of quite amazing proportions. 'I don't see that there's any need for sarcasm or ridicule, and as,' she continued haughtily, 'you gave no indication on how or where I am to be spending the next two days, I had to guess at the sort of thing to wear.' She glared at him as he walked around to her side of the car, after stowing away her luggage, and opened the passenger door.

'Me, sarcastic? Perish the thought!' he drawled smoothly. 'And risk the ferocity of Miss King's displeasure?' He shook his head, a derisive smile twitching the corner of his mouth. 'Time is passing, Miss King; get in. Oh, and try to take that scowl off your face.' He placed a guiding hand on Christy's back. 'It's giving the neighbours something to talk about.' He raised a hand and waved to a window two doors along and a bedroom curtain fell swiftly back into place. 'You see,' he added as he got back into the Ferrari, 'this area isn't any different from all the rest—there are nosy old bats like that one wherever you happen to live.'

'That woman happens to be a baroness!' Christy retorted sharply. 'She's hardly an old bat.'

Drew started the car and the engine roared into powerful life. 'Well, nosy old baroness, then,' he amended easily, stretching the seatbelt across his broad chest. 'As I said, there's very little difference.'

'That's just the sort of remark I would have expected from you,' Christy replied, as she fastened herself in. 'Typical! And for your information, if I want to scowl for the whole of the time I have to suffer your company, I will—OK?'

The broad, rugged frame beside her shrugged with obvious unconcern. 'Your choice. But don't you think it's going to be rather a long forty-eight hours?'

Christy cast a sideways glance and glared at the strongly shaped profile. 'It's going to be eternity whatever I do,' she replied with a sweet smile. 'So what's the point in trying to hide my deeper feelings? Scowling comes naturally when you're anywhere in my vicinity.' She paused momentarily, and then added, 'Unless you haven't worked it out already, Mr Drew Michaels, I'll say it now loud and clear, just so we both know where we are—I don't happen to like you.'

She was dying to see a reaction, an indication that she had annoyed him, angered him, hurt his pride, that ego which so often afflicted big stars in the worst kind of way. Christy watched and waited and saw little, except evidence of that brand of patronising amusement that was usually reserved for silly young children who didn't know any better.

'Oh, I think I've worked that one out all right.' Drew's mouth widened as he manoeuvred the car through the heavy London traffic. 'And all by myself too, and, just so we both know where we stand, let me say now that I'm not too impressed by you either.' He turned cold eyes upon her. 'Did you see the articles in the gossip columns relating to our little contretemps in the restaurant last week, by the way?'

'No!' Christy replied snappily, turning to gaze out of the window. 'I did not.'

'Probably just as well,' Drew replied cuttingly. 'You did come out of it looking rather...' he paused and pretended to struggle for the right word '...ridiculous? But then I know you have quite a strength of character. You do, I'm sure, get over such embarrassing set-backs.' His mouth curled tauntingly. 'The various snippets were rather unkind. Such a shame, I thought, the way they seemed to ridicule you. And Conrad, poor, innocent bystander that he was, got roped in rather badly too.' He paused and then added in tones that had 'wind up' written all over them, 'I mean, you only have to look at the man to see that he's not nearly as much of a wimp as they made out.'

'He's more of a man than you'll ever be!' Christy responded with unthinking fervour. She glanced angrily across and saw Drew's mocking expression far too late.

'A tiger in bed?' he quipped icily. 'Well, aren't you the lucky one?'

'I didn't say that!' Christy snapped, her eyes blazing. 'Typical, though, of you to bring the conversation down to that level. Conrad happens to be a good friend, that's all! And besides, I don't judge a true man on how he happens to perform between the sheets. It doesn't make one iota of difference to me.'

Drew raised one dark, disbelieving brow. 'No?'

'No!' Her cheeks felt hot. She surreptitiously placed long, manicured fingers against her skin and hoped to goodness he hadn't noticed her flush of embarrassment.

'Not a subject you wish to discuss, I see.' Drew glanced across with an infuriating smile at Christy's uncomfortable expression. 'So why's that? Either Conrad's an abject failure in bed, or the poor devil hasn't been given the opportunity to prove himself one way or the other. Which is it, Christy? I find I'm really quite intrigued.'

'You're a coarse rat, aren't you?' she shot back angrily, turning towards him. 'And downright disgusting! And if you imagine for one second that I would even begin to reveal parts of my personal life to you, you're——'

'You've revealed more than aspects of your personal life to me—or has that rather passionate moment in time slipped from your memory?' he asked, with deliberate bluntness.

So, just a few minutes into the weekend and he had already decided to throw that at her! She stared sideways as the Ferrari overtook a black taxi cab and forced herself to keep cool. 'I cut all memory of that great mistake from my mind the moment I left the hotel bedroom!' she informed him icily. 'As far as I'm concerned it was a totally forgettable experience!'

Drew turned and cast observant blue eyes over Christy's flushed, angry face. 'So why are you so uptight, then? Tell me that.'

Forty-eight hours of this? Christy thought angrily. I'm going to go mad at least a dozen times over! 'I'm not uptight!' she snapped haughtily. 'And... and——' she steeled herself '—and if you think that the fact that we had brief, unmeaning sex once three years ago has any bearing now on how I feel, then your ego is bigger than I estimated! Look, I'll make it plain now, shall I, Mr Michaels?' she added with force. 'I'm here because I've signed a contract for this series and under the terms of that ludicrous piece of paper I have to undertake to interview you. I am a professional and, as much as I would prefer to be doing other things, such as spring-cleaning my house, shopping for mundane items, or even washing my hair, I will endeavour to carry out the terms of my contract to the full. However, in no area of small print does it say that I have to like the people I interview. I will of course be civil at all times——'

'Civil?' He laughed out loud, filling the confined interior of the car with an infectious sound that in any other circumstances would have been incredibly pleasing.

Christy turned her head away, annoyed beyond belief that he should be so genuinely amused, so unperturbed by what she had just said. She hadn't wanted to refer to that time, but to allow him to think for just one moment that what had happened then did in any way mean anything to her...

She took a deep breath, refusing to acknowledge for even a second that Drew Michaels looked more gorgeous than ever, when his eyes crinkled with laughter and his mouth broadened to reveal strong, incredibly white teeth.

'Well, I must say,' he continued when his mirth had subsided a little, 'that I'm looking forward to seeing you when you're really angry. Will a mere man survive the wrath of Christy King, do you suppose?'

'I will of course be civil,' she continued determinedly, keeping her gaze fixed out of the side-window, 'but you will be sorely disappointed if you hope for any sort of atmosphere, other than——'

'OK. OK, I get the picture.' Drew changed through the gears and turned off a busy main road. 'You're spending time with me under sufferance and if I expect the same sort of response as last time——'

'You're going to be sorely disappointed!' Christy finished for him in crisp tones. 'I never make the same mistake twice, Mr Michaels; you want to remember that.'

'You don't consider this a mistake, then—agreeing to spend two days solely in my company?' he enquired tauntingly.

She felt a lurch of trepidation and knew instantly that it *was* a mistake, and a very big one at that. God, she had been an absolute fool to imagine for one moment that she could get the better of this man. 'W-why should I?' she managed carelessly. 'As I made plain before, I'm here to do——'

'Yes. I know.' He turned and curved his lips into a contemptuous smile. 'You're here to do a job.'

'Where exactly are we going?'

They had been travelling for some miles. The question of her destination hadn't occurred to her before now—she had been too busy fuming over all that he had said. But earlier this morning it had been the first thing she had promised herself she would ask.

'Wait and see.' He reached forward and pressed the car's CD player into action.

'And if I don't wish to?' Christy replied stiffly, trying her best to be heard above the thumping, incessant beat of heavy rock, which was reverberating throughout the car's suddenly claustrophobic interior. 'I would like to know where we're going now.'

'Well, you'll just have to wait to find out, because right at this moment I don't care to enlighten you.' He glanced carelessly across and threw her a glittering look. 'Let's just keep it as a surprise, shall we?'

As the miles passed, Christy became more and more intrigued as to where Drew Michaels was driving them both. All the reasonable, most likely possibilities were knocked off her mental list one by one, and as the Ferrari began to make its way along a dusty track she had to fight against her natural curiosity and feign complete and utter uninterest. After Drew's last remark, she had decided that unless speech was absolutely necessary she would play dumb all the way. Besides, battling against the music would have been almost impossible anyway. And after all, what did it matter where they were going? she thought irritably. If he wanted to play silly little games then that was up to him...

The light aircraft looked too small and too fragile. Christy sat staring at it through the windscreen of the parked Ferrari and wondered if Drew Michaels was enjoying the effects of producing this, his trump card.

'Come along, Miss King, time to get out. I have your bag and your equipment.'

She swallowed with difficulty, aware that her throat had suddenly turned as dry as a desert, and immediately began to rummage in her handbag. 'I...I just need to fix my face.' With shaking hands she fumbled for the soft coral lipstick she had chosen to wear with her outfit and attempted to look as if she meant what she said.

Drew heaved an exasperated sigh. 'Your lips look perfect, your face looks perfect, in fact your whole body looks absolutely gorgeous, as you very well know. Now forget your face and hurry up! I want to get going before the weather changes. The forecast isn't too good for later on today...'

Christy listened to the last sentence with a sinking heart, immediately visualising the prospect of flying goodness knew where in a flimsy light aircraft with thunder and lightning and wind and turbulence and all the other awful possibilities that always sprang to mind whenever the prospect of flying loomed into view.

Did he know how much she detested it? she wondered, as she doggedly began powdering her nose. Was he really planning to take her up in the sky in that thing, simply to get his own back, to make her suffer?

The small round compact mirror reflected her sudden pale complexion. Christy snapped it shut and glanced up into his face, her large violet eyes wide with sudden anxiety. What to do? Refuse point-blank without an explanation? Tell him? She shook her head involuntarily. And give him the ammunition to parade that weakness in front of her? She glanced over to the stationary aircraft. If only it hadn't been so small. Getting into jumbo jets had taken her two years of determined self-will and discipline; only recently had she started to feel any amount of confidence about trusting herself to the skies. But in this thing?

'Am I allowed to know where you plan to take me now?' she asked in a voice that was surprisingly firm, surprisingly cool and controlled, despite everything.

'Don't look so worried, Miss King; you make it sound as if I'm kidnapping you at the very least!' Drew slanted her a slightly puzzled look. 'We're just going up to Scotland. I have a particularly beautiful old farmhouse there, right on the edges of a loch.'

Scotland. Was that good? Christy wondered, desperately trying to find some crumb of comfort on which to hold. Well, at least they weren't going to cross the Channel; there would be firm ground below them for all of the way.

She found herself gazing into his face, surveying the stunning, dark features, picturing the contemptuous curve of the lips that would surely appear if she told him how frightened she was at the prospect of flying.

You're going to do it. The voice was small and unsure, but it was there deep inside forcing her on. You must. There is no way you are going to allow this ridiculous phobia to get the better of you. You are going to be strong and composed and you are not going to allow Drew Michaels to have any suspicions at all.

Her legs felt like jelly as she got out of the car and waited while he locked it up. Crossing the tarmac was like living a nightmare, watching as the plane became larger and larger, but still, as far as Christy was concerned, not large enough.

She was so preoccupied with keeping her fear at a controllable level and her composure intact that it wasn't until Drew was actually strapping himself in beside her that she realised that it was he that was going to pilot the plane.

'You fly?' Her voice didn't sound quite normal, but he seemed not to notice.

'Yes, that's right.'

Christy watched nervously as he placed dark glasses on his nose, a pair of headphones over his thick dark hair, and began to check the dials in front of him.

'How long?'

'Oh, I got my licence just last week; I'm looking forward to having a practice.'

Christy felt the colour drain from her face. This couldn't really be happening, could it? Practice? She stared ahead out of the window and thought about backing out, telling him she just couldn't go through with the flight. So what if she looked a complete fool? It had happened before, hadn't it? She had survived.

Out of the corner of her eye she saw Drew glance across. 'Are you feeling OK?' His dark brows were drawn together slightly and Christy saw a vague expression of concern shadowing his face. 'Look, I was only kidding before,' he added carelessly, handing her some headphones. 'I've actually been flying for ten years now. I have more flying hours under my belt than I care to remember so you've no need to worry.'

'Who said I was worried?' Christy arched surprised eyebrows and tried to play the part of someone totally in control. 'I'm just not particularly enamored about flying all the way to Scotland, that's all!'

'Why not? It's a very beautiful country.'

He flicked numerous switches, checked dials and then before she knew what was happening the engine roared into life. Christy swallowed back the lump in her throat and hastily fastened her seatbelt.

Too late, she thought, surreptitiously gripping the seat as the aircraft taxied along the runway. You can't tell him now, you stupid girl!

She felt the prickle of fear, the sudden sickness in the pit of her stomach as the plane got up speed and closed her eyes tightly as the aircraft lurched into the cloudless blue sky. When she finally found the courage to open them again, she realised he was watching her.

'You should have told me you were petrified of flying,' he commented with aggravating superiority. 'We could have driven.'

'And put up with travelling in a car for six hours with you!' Christy's voice was noticeably wobbly, but she was pleased with her retort. If he thought she was going to go all soft on him, just because she had a small problem with flying, then he had another think coming. She cleared her throat and struggled like mad to look as if she was handling the fact that they were goodness knew how many thousands of feet above the ground perfectly well.

'Are you interested in knowing how long it will take to get to our destination? Or would that just add to your torture?'

Christy pursed her lips and tried to work out where she should focus her gaze. His face was out of the question—those handsome, assured, mocking features were more than she could bear right now, and there seemed to be an awful lot of window, revealing an expanse of countryside that was far too far below. She stared determinedly down at her hands, clenched tightly together in her lap. 'You're enjoying every moment of my discomfort, aren't you?' she accused bitterly.

'You don't honestly believe that?' His voice was light, but there was a faintly incredulous undertone, as if the fact that she did was somehow shocking to him. 'Actually I have every sympathy,' he continued, when she made no reply. 'It must be pretty awful. Well done. You're handling it very well.'

I'm not, she thought. I think I'm going to throw up any minute. Out loud she said in rather a pitiful, small voice, 'A compliment—from you? Surely I must be hearing things!'

'It has been known. Try and look out of the window,' he suggested after a moment; 'you'll feel better. Go on, do it, Christy. There's nothing to be afraid of.'

She hesitated a moment, struggling against her automatic negative response, reeling from the fact that unless she was hallucinating Drew Michaels had actually complimented her, spoken to her in a voice that held something approaching admiration, used her first name and made it sound like honey on his lips—just like last time.

She swallowed and felt her throat dry with fear and then she raised her head slowly, almost cautiously, and did as she was told, taking a deep breath as her eyes focused on the view ahead.

'See, not so bad, is it?'

She took some more breaths, worked on calming herself and then nodded very slightly.

'Do you go through this every time you fly?' Drew asked, glancing across at Christy's still pale face.

She shook her head and found herself meeting his dark gaze for the first time since they had taken off. 'I've just never been in a light aircraft before,' she murmured. 'It's all much more real, isn't it? You're not so insulated. I mean,' Christy explained breathlessly, 'when I fly in a jumbo, after the initial take-off at least, I can just about convince myself, if I work at it very hard, that I'm not travelling by air at all. Here...' she paused and gulped, and looked down at the patchwork view below for a brief second '...well, there's just no getting away from it, is there?'

'So, are you looking forward to doing this series of interviews?' Drew asked after a moment, changing the subject, she suspected, to take her mind off things. 'Present company excluded, of course.'

'Oh...well, yes. Yes, I am.' It took Christy a second to put her thoughts back into work mode.

He turned and slanted dark brows at her. 'You don't sound too sure about it,' he commented drily. 'I thought this new project was your baby. Haven't you been the one working like mad to make it happen?'

'You seem to be very well informed,' Christy replied coolly, gathering her professional wits back again, reminding herself with irritation that she had somehow allowed things to slide far too far already.

'Oh, I have my sources.'

'Did they suggest you invite yourself on the list of interviewees?' she risked enquiring. 'You, I believe, approached the producer yourself, isn't that correct?'

He smiled across at her. A self-satisfied, infuriating smile that reminded Christy why it was she couldn't stand him. 'Oh, quite right. Of course when I heard that you were the one doing the interviewing...' Drew shrugged, his eyes dancing. 'Well, I just felt I couldn't pass the opportunity by—after all, we had such a lot of fun last time, didn't we?'

She ignored the goading tone, the look of absolute devilment in his eyes. 'Not to mention the fact,' she added crisply, 'that you have another book which you're working on, which will be released at about the same time these series of interviews will be broadcast.'

His lips curled. 'Never even came into it.'

She heaved an infuriated sigh, closed her eyes with resolute determination and made a vow not to utter another word until they had reached the end of their journey.

Christy didn't exactly sleep—that would have been asking too much—but she did sort of drift, doze into a semi-oblivious state. She had had rather a late night, rather too many late nights in fact, and as her situation became more familiar to her, as the early summer sun warmed the cockpit to rather a pleasant temperature, she found she was more able to relax than she ever would have dreamt one hour ago.

The fact that *he* was sitting only inches from her was the most difficult thing to overcome. Christy was far more aware than she wanted to be of Drew's almost overpowering male presence beside her.

She wondered, not for the first time, how it was she allowed him to produce such strong negative emotions in her. It had been—to coin a phrase—an extremely brief encounter, something she should have got over, forgotten, and she *had* enjoyed a reasonably lengthy, if tame relationship with Conrad since that time; it hadn't marred her for life, falling into bed on the spur of the moment, it hadn't scarred her very soul or anything, had it? Logically, she simply couldn't produce an adequate explanation. So he had ruined her credibility on that show three years ago? The viewing public, by and large, had forgotten the incident, the hierarchy of television big guns had seen the knock-on effect, been surprised and happy about the fact that more people had tuned in to watch after that—he had in a perverse kind of way done her a weird sort of favour. So why did she still let him get to her?

A sudden jolt and then a stomach-lurching sensation as the plane dropped many, many feet had

Christy forgetting the question instantly as she opened her eyes in horror.

The sun was nowhere to be seen now, no blue skies at all, just grey-black clouds totally obliterating any possible view. It was as if they had entered another world.

Christy closed her eyes in despair and then opened them again swiftly, praying that the scene would have somehow miraculously changed. She glanced across at Drew, watched, her brows knitted together in alarm, as he fought to keep the plane under control.

Somehow, he managed a moment to look across and give a reassuring smile. It made quite a difference, but nothing, not even so attractive and reassuring a gesture as that, could dispel the rising panic and dread that was growing inside Christy with every second that passed.

'It's just a storm. We'll get through it.' Drew's voice was perfectly calm—too calm perhaps? Christy risked a sideways glance out of the plane; her body was already rigid with fear and she wished she hadn't. It looked dreadful. It felt dreadful.

'Are . . . ?' She swallowed and licked at her dry lips, tasting the familiar coral lipstick. 'Are we nearly there?'

Drew nodded, his brows drawn together in concentration, his large capable hands fixed on the wheel. 'Not far. There's going to be quite a bit more turbulence before we're through this, though, so hang on tight.' He turned and smiled again, a relaxed, sympathetic smile. Christy hung on to it, placed every last ounce of faith in this man's capabilities to get them both through.

When the thunder and lightning started, Christy gripped the seat, closed her eyes and just prayed. It seemed to go on forever, but when finally she opened them again the skies were several shades lighter, there was little rain and the buffeting had halted completely. She breathed an audible sigh and vowed immediately that she'd never set foot in an aeroplane again. 'Thank goodness for that!' She peered cautiously out through the window and scanned the wild open countryside below for signs of life, for signs that they were there—wherever 'there' was. 'Is it far now?' she asked, slight impatience creeping into her voice.

She felt better, stronger. If she could survive that, she felt she could survive almost anything. 'Well?' Some of the old asperity was returning. 'I asked if there was much further to go.'

'Not far.' His voice was tight, full of tension.

If Christy had been paying attention, maybe, just maybe, she would have detected the change in tone immediately, noticed the contrast in atmosphere that pervaded the cockpit. As it was all she could think about was the fact that she had survived, that soon her feet would be on beautiful solid ground.

'Is there something wrong?' Her voice was barely more than a whisper two minutes later. She *knew* something was amiss now; she felt it; watching Drew for the last few seconds, seeing his alert body, feeling the tension that exuded from each of his movements told her that there was a problem. No storm now, but something else, something infinitely worse?

'I'm going to have to land the plane. Make sure you're strapped in well. Do you know the emergency landing position?'

Christy's eyes widened with horror. 'What are you——?'

'For once in your life stop arguing and just do it!' he commanded, in tones that made her tremble. 'Knees together, head forward, elbows locked in tight. And don't look so panic-stricken; it's going to be all right.'

And it was. Drew undoubtedly was a most experienced pilot. Christy felt a tremendous bump and suddenly they were down safely on terra firma, none the worse for the swift, unforeseen descent.

The track was straight and long. Christy raised her head and released her grip on her seat a little as the plane gradually slowed to a halt.

'So what happens now?' she asked shakily. 'What on earth are we supposed to do?'

CHAPTER FOUR

'ARE you OK?'

Christy glanced into the handsome, tanned face and bit down on her bottom lip to stop it trembling.

'Oh, great, just perfect!' she replied waspishly, rubbing at a vague pain in her leg and trying to feel brave and in control, trying to ignore the fact that she wanted to howl out loud. 'Don't fuss! I'm fine,' she added, brushing away the large tanned hand that was, she felt sure, about to examine her aching knee. Her eyes skimmed over Drew's face and she pursed her lips resolutely. It was difficult sustaining the anger but she had to do it. To allow anything else to take hold at this moment would be absolute folly. If she started to cry now, she didn't think she would be able to stop.

She ran a shaky hand over her face and took a few intense breaths. 'I can't believe this is happening,' she murmured haltingly, aware that her voice sounded feeble and weak. She took a deep breath and fought like mad to keep some degree of coolness and detachment in her tone. 'What on earth did we have to land for? The plane's all right surely?'

'Oh, it's fine!' Drew murmured drily, glancing out of the cockpit window. 'I like making unexpected landings in the middle of nowhere—I always find it adds spice to a trip!'

'You know what I mean!' Christy retorted shakily. 'And don't talk to me as if I'm a child! So what is wrong with it, then?' she added swiftly. 'One moment we were up and the next . . . the next . . .' She pressed her hands firmly into her lap and forced her voice to sound hard and practical. 'Was it the engine, or something to do with the storm?'

'Does it matter what it was?' Drew murmured, slipping the headset around his neck. 'We're down now and there's not a lot we can do about it.'

'I like to know things,' Christy replied firmly. 'Stop treating me like an imbecile!'

Drew's voice was crisp. 'OK, if you really want to know, the engine was starved of fuel. There must be a blockage somewhere.'

'But you can fix it?' Her voice, she knew, sounded pathetically hopeful.

'No.' Drew stretched his arms above his head. 'I don't have any tools.'

'Oh, just great! I suppose that would be too much to expect,' Christy retorted irritably. 'Too simple, too easy, far too straightforward! So where exactly are we?' she added stiffly, glancing around. 'Or is that a ridiculous question? I don't suppose you have the faintest idea, do you? Hell! Just look out there.' She gestured through the cockpit window at the impressive view ahead of them. She could feel the tears welling up inside again. The shock, she supposed. A reaction to the whole absolutely unexpected situation. 'Look at all this . . . this wilderness! We're stranded, aren't we? Miles from anywhere——' Her voice was rising. It sounded strained; her throat felt tight from battling against the tears.

'You can cut out the hysterics right now!' Drew ordered curtly. 'Getting worked up isn't going to help matters! Now make yourself useful and pass me that map,' he rasped, 'and concentrate on keeping that de-

lectable mouth of yours shut. I don't feel in any mood
to handle overwrought females at this moment.'

'I am not an overwrought female!' Christy stormed.

'Oh, no?' Drew threw her a withering look. 'Well,
you're giving a pretty good impression in that case.'

'So how on earth do you expect me to act?' she
demanded. 'We're lost in the middle of some remote
part of Scotland, and you tell me not to get worked
up!'

'Are you going to continue with this?' Drew demanded savagely, lifting his head suddenly from the
map to glare at her. 'For God's sake, can't you understand how lucky we've been?' He released a breath,
and dragged strong fingers through his dark, springy
hair. 'No, obviously you can't. Look, just sit quietly
while I study this map and be thankful for small
mercies, will you?'

'I don't feel like being thankful for small mercies!'
Christy retorted, eyes flashing. 'I feel like being upset
and angry, because you made me fly in this damn
plane and you were the one who assured me everything was going to be all right and you were going to
handle everything. Well, it wasn't and you didn't!'

She felt the tears welling up in her eyes and swiftly
she ripped off the headset and jerked open the door.

'Christy!' She heard his tone of exasperation and
was immediately angry with herself for becoming
emotional, weak, all the things she hated. Drew leaned
over and grabbed her arm. 'Pull yourself together!
It's not as bad as all that.' He tugged her back towards
him determinedly. 'Look, I know this has been hard
for you. You hate flying and us having to land like
this...well, it can't have been easy. But there's nothing
to worry about. Nothing.'

'Oh, no?' Christy's voice shook a little, portraying just a little of her uncertainty.

'No.' Drew's voice was sure and confident. 'Trust me,' he demanded. 'Just calm down and trust me.'

She felt his arm across her bent shoulders, was aware of the pure masculine smell of him—a mixture of fresh soap and clean body scent. For a brief moment she had a compulsion to turn towards Drew, to succumb and allow herself to be held. He looked so sure, every part of him exuding masculine strength. Christy took a breath and closed her eyes for a brief moment. Trust him? Was she mad even to consider it? 'Let me go!' Her voice was harsh as she jerked free from his hold. 'I . . . I need to get out of here. I need some fresh air.'

She surreptitiously wiped at her glistening eyes with the back of her hand and surveyed the scene in front of her with a sinking heart, despite the fact that the view ahead was incredible. Mile after mile of craggy Scottish moorland, dipping and winding its way through a valley of spectacular proportions. A gurgling stream rushed down a hillside just a few yards away to her right. Glades of trees, she hadn't a clue what, fringed the faster, wider river ahead that must surely at some point meet the sea. It was truly a scene of breathtaking beauty. A scene that at this moment made Christy feel sick, hate every last inch of it, because there wasn't one sign of life and that meant she would be imprisoned here with Drew Michaels for longer than she cared even to contemplate.

'So how are we supposed to get out of this hell-hole and back to civilisation?' She spun round as he emerged from the plane and managed to produce a scowl that matched the tone of her voice. 'As far as

I can see, there's nothing for miles and miles. Certainly no convenient hire car outlets, no bus-stops.'

Drew raised dark brows. 'Ever heard of walking?' he enquired with matching heavy sarcasm. 'Or don't exclusive television celebrities like yourself have to do that any more?'

'So where exactly are we going to walk to?' Christy asked crisply, forcing herself to ignore his infuriating retort. She threw him a humourless smile and continued before he could reply, 'I know, don't tell me! This is all some sort of macabre practical joke. Around the edge of that slight incline, nestling in a pretty little hollow, is your luxury retreat, complete with telephone, fast car, everything, in fact, that we could possibly need! Go on! Tell me!' she demanded fiercely, almost desperately. 'Say it's true.'

Drew shrugged and leant back against the nose of the plane, looking at her with that unfathomable expression that always made Christy's blood boil. 'I wish I could,' he remarked grimly, 'then I wouldn't have to endure your particular brand of not very witty sarcasm. You really do like to make the most of a situation, don't you?'

'And just what is that supposed to mean?' Christy flashed angrily.

'Histrionics are never particularly becoming,' Drew replied bitingly, 'especially when they're performed by women who are usually perfectly capable of control.'

'Well, I'm so sorry if my reactions aren't to your taste, but they feel appropriate in the circumstances!' Christy snapped. 'I suppose you would prefer a weak, emotionally dependent little woman! Someone who felt totally confident in your abilities. Who just said, Yes, Drew, no Drew, three bags full, Drew!'

'No. But I'd be content with someone who didn't insist on throwing tantrums, who didn't act like a spoilt little schoolgirl, just because something's not gone to plan!' he snarled. 'There's little point in getting this uptight, you know that, don't you?' he added coldly, watching with infuriating coolness as Christy walked up and down, hands on hips. 'It's not going to help matters. It won't change the fact that you and I are going to have to spend a certain amount of time together tramping across miles of Scottish countryside.'

Christy folded her arms and schooled her expression to show no hint of weakness. Spoilt schoolgirl! How dared he? How dared he lounge there as if everything were under control, as if she were making a fuss for *nothing*? They had just had to land in the middle of nowhere, for God's sake!

'And you can take that haughty expression off your face right now, Christy. It doesn't impress me in the slightest.'

'Impress you!' She put all the scorn she could into her voice. 'Why on earth would I want to do that? Look, I just want to get out of here and——'

He moved before she had finished her sentence. Christy struggled to hold her ground. He was struggling to keep a hold of his temper. She saw the dangerous glint in the steely eyes and wished she had had the sense to keep quiet. Making Drew Michaels angry at a time like this was not a very clever move, she thought belatedly.

He looked mad, more mad than she had ever seen him. His eyes flashed fire. Christy gasped a breath and made as if to move. 'Stay where you are!' he ordered savagely. 'Don't you dare move a muscle!'

She licked nervously at her lips and tried to tilt her chin in an attitude of vague defiance. 'Playing the macho man again, Drew——?'

'Cut it out!' Drew glowered down at her. 'Listen, Christy, and listen good. You may be able to talk to your friends, your colleagues at work, the poor devils who come into contact with you every day like that, but not to me. No one—*no one*,' he repeated with savage emphasis, 'talks to me like that, least of all you, got it? Well?' He reached out and dragged her close towards him with one rough jerk of his arm. 'Look at me! *Have you got that*?'

Christy trembled, staring up into the dark, angry face, registering the taut mouth, the fierce expression in the steely eyes, and nodded briefly.

'I'm in charge,' Drew continued bluntly, 'and from this moment onwards you do as I say. I want no more of this egotistical performance. Now I'm going to radio in our position. Make sure you stay here and don't do something stupid like wandering off!'

She watched him go, saw the violent way he wrenched open the plane's door and then as she felt her legs turn to jelly she sank to the ground. It had been a powerful onslaught and it had produced the desired effect. Christy felt numb with shock.

'How . . . how long will they be?'

'Who?' She saw the dark brows draw together irritably and wondered whether she had said too much already.

'The . . . the rescue services—that is who you were contacting?' She managed something approaching a small smile. 'Silly of me, but I forgot all about the radio.' She held her breath, feeling suddenly very tiny and insignificant, and stared hopefully up at the broad figure.

'I radioed in our position,' Drew replied crisply, 'but if you're hoping for some kind of dramatic rescue I'm afraid you're going to be disappointed.'

'What?' Christy clambered to her feet. She shook her head in disbelief. 'But surely...I mean for goodness' sakes we're stranded here miles from no-where——' Her voice was rising. 'We've got to be rescued.'

'We don't need to waste the time of the emergency services. We're in good shape. I know where we are——'

'You may but I surely don't——' Christy began.

'And,' Drew continued with a warning look, 'I'm in charge. We walk.'

Christy watched him turn and march back to the plane. How could this be happening? she thought with something approaching despair. What have I done to deserve this...this agony? Her eyes skimmed the rugged male torso, the broad line of Drew's shoulders and all at once she felt a sudden, desolate pang of loneliness. The prospect of what might possibly lay ahead...the thought of spending time alone with hateful, domineering Drew Michaels among all this countryside, all this nature! She knew she just wouldn't be able to cope.

Christy shook her head despairingly. She desperately wanted to argue about his decision. Why did they have to walk? She still couldn't see the point. 'Drew...please, I——' She hurried over to the plane.

'Here, it's pretty much intact.' Drew thrust the leather holdall at her.

'What . . . what about my recording equipment? Is that OK?'

Drew rewarded her with a look of vague contempt, a slow mocking smile curving the arrogant mouth. 'As I'm not about to offer you an interview right now, I don't think it matters at this particular moment. Or were you planning on lugging it all the way?'

'Now who's being sarcastic?' Christy retorted angrily. She snatched at her holdall and carried it a short distance away, kneeling down on the dry, springy grass to examine the contents. It didn't make her feel any better. No invaluable hooded weatherproof coat, no thick jumper, no practical hiking boots, not even a pair of jeans.

Christy bit absent-mindedly at a manicured finger-nail and then glanced down at her cream linen trousers. They would be ruined! She shook her head despondently. She hated this place. Why couldn't she be back at home in her wonderfully comfortable three-storey town house? Or with friends? Cathy and Paul had invited her over to their place in the south of France for the weekend. She could have been on a yacht now in the French Riviera soaking up the sun. Why here, with a leg that ached unbearably, a dreadful headache that thumped as if it were fit to burst, feeling cold and—the latest torture—suddenly very hungry?

She cursed as she rummaged through the carefully folded items and retrieved an elegant crocheted cardigan that matched the trousers she was wearing. Not suitable at all, but it was better than nothing. She shrugged it over her cream silk blouse, pulling it tight across her breasts, and glanced up at the sky. It looked ominously dark. 'Please don't rain!' she pleaded quietly to the rolling black clouds. 'I couldn't cope.'

'I see you've found something more suitable to wear.'

Christy let out a taut breath at the sound of his scornful tone and looked up, spearing him with a look that would have made many a man flinch. Not Drew Michaels, though.

'Are you cold?'

'Just a little chilly,' Christy replied haughtily, 'I'm fine now, thank you.'

'Only I've got a spare jumper if you're interested.' He held it out, almost taunting her with the soft, thick, far more practical green cashmere sweater. 'I'm quite willing to lend it, if you wish.'

'I'll be fine,' Christy repeated determinedly, looking away from the faintly smiling mouth, vowing as she did so that she would have to be on the verge of frostbite before she gave in and asked him for it.

'If you're sure?' he murmured, tying the garment casually around his waist.

'Have we got to go far?' Christy tried to make her voice sound casual, as if the prospect of trekking goodness knew how many miles were of only slight interest to her. 'There doesn't seem to be anything for as far as the eye can see, does there? And it's——' She paused and looked at her slim gold wristwatch. 'It's almost two o'clock.'

'This track leads through the valley down there. We'll follow it. According to the map there's a farm at the end of it.'

Christy arched a well-shaped brow. 'And if there's no one there?'

Drew lifted his broad shoulders in a casual shrug. 'We find somewhere else.'

She hesitated a moment and then said, 'This is ridiculous; we could be out of here in half an hour.'

'We are walking!' He slammed the door of the plane hard shut. 'My God, you really don't know when to keep quiet, do you?' His eyes sparked dangerously and Christy cursed her own foolishness once again. 'We walk, Christy, and you can like it or lump it.'

She glanced, fuming, at his angular features and made it look as if she was considering her options. The fact that she had none was, she knew, clear to them both.

'OK, I'll walk,' she said at last.

Drew smiled coldly. 'That, Christy, as you very well know, has never been in question. Now, there are a couple of things that I've still to get and then we'll set off.'

He returned in less than a couple of minutes with a small haversack slung over one shoulder. Christy picked up her own bulky holdall and resolutely began walking down the track.

'You're not honestly planning to take that thing!'

She spun back around and saw that his glance was scornful—as ever, Christy thought angrily. 'And why not?' She pursed her lips and gripped the handle of her bag ever tighter. 'It's got all my things in. You're taking something.'

He gave her a look of something approaching complete bemusement. For a moment Christy thought he was going to order her to leave the holdall in the plane. Instead he held up his hands in an impatient gesture, as if allowing the inevitable to take its course. 'OK! Suit yourself,' he said tersely. 'Just don't expect me to carry it when you find that it's breaking your arms off, that's all.'

'Don't worry!' Christy retorted, marching ahead of him down the dusty incline. 'I wouldn't ask for your help, not even if I were on my last legs!'

What a parting shot. How positive she had sounded. What a pity that just as she uttered the last syllable her legs gave way beneath her on the deceptively slippery stony surface and sent her tumbling for all of ten feet on her firm, well-shaped rear. She shrieked instinctively, her face red with horror and extreme embarrassment as she came to an undignified, extremely dusty stop.

She sat, legs sprawled out in front of her, and closed her eyes in absolute frustration. She had a sudden overwhelming notion to yell and stamp her feet, just as she used to do when she was a child. What is happening to me? she wondered incomprehensibly. What am I doing?

She heard the thud of following footsteps and soon Drew was beside her. 'You dropped your bag.' With a solemn air he held out the holdall that had left her grasp at the first moment of her fall, his expression perfectly straight.

'Don't you dare laugh!' Christy ground out threateningly, knowing that beneath that sombre expression he was bursting his sides with amusement. 'It's not funny.'

'And if I think it is?' he questioned. 'If I dare to laugh because for once Christy King looks just a little silly?'

She glared at him, breathing hard, aware that there was a sudden unmistakable note of challenge in his voice. What *would* she do if he laughed? What *could* she do?

'I don't like people laughing at me,' she managed breathlessly.

Drew raised an eyebrow, his mouth twisting slightly at one corner. 'Why not?'

Christy glanced into the ruggedly handsome face and then swiftly down at her hands.

At the children's home, she had always been the one that was laughed at. In those days, long, long ago now, she had been small and skinny, with hair that was long and unkempt, and the bigger girls had poked and pulled her and taunted her unbearably...

Christy absent-mindedly lifted a hand and touched the gleaming golden mane that whipped around her shoulders in the breeze. Children could be so cruel, she thought. Even now it hurt her to think back. She held her hand out for the bag. 'Laugh, then, if you must,' she told him carelessly, 'but just give me my holdall.'

'And if I don't choose to?'

She glanced sharply across at him, registering his change of tone, noting an expression on his face that she didn't quite understand. 'The trappings of wealth mean a lot to you, don't they, Christy?' he continued quietly, holding the bag tantalisingly out of reach. 'The items in here, what they represent, the designer clothes, the expensive perfume, even the bag it-self——' he examined it properly for the first time '—made by Gucci—even this—they're a comfort to you, aren't they? Just like...' He paused a moment, searching for a description that was to his taste. 'Like a child who has to carry round a blanket for comfort. Who——'

'How dare you?' Christy's eyes were blazing as she scrambled to her feet. 'Just who the hell do you think

you are, talking to me like this? A comfort blanket?'
She shook her head and released a short, harsh laugh.
'I don't quite see your line of comparison, Mr
Michaels,' she enunciated crisply. 'For your information, the things in that bag happen to cost a damn
sight more than some scrap of rag that a child chooses
to carry around!'

'You mean you're going to go to the trouble of
lugging that thing with you just because the items in
it cost a few hundred pounds?'

'And is there something wrong with that?' Christy
challenged. 'Is there something wrong with looking
after your possessions, cherishing them? Just because
you seem to have no qualms about leaving several
thousand pounds' worth of light aircraft——!'

She knew she had gone too far. Knew the tension
that always existed between them had reached that
point of no return as soon as Drew threw down the
bag and dragged Christy into his arms. It happened
so quickly. One minute she was in full verbal swing,
preparing to launch into an attack that she hoped
would match his insulting psychiatric claptrap, the
next she felt the full force of his mouth on hers, the
taste of lips that were strong and sure and demanding.

The shock of his actions stilled Christy into sub-
servience. She really couldn't believe he was daring
to do this. She hated him. He knew that. And yet he
had the gall to kiss her!

His hands were pulling her closer as his lips explored her partially open mouth, securing her within
his strong, suntanned arms. His body was like a rock,
all muscle, all powerful, yet somehow he was holding
her with infinite gentleness—firmly, yes, but without
the brute force she maybe would have expected.

How long since she had been kissed like this? The question scorched her mind, let itself be known up and down every square inch of her body as his lazy, hungry mouth, the sensitive exploring hands produced an effect that was infinitely shocking. He was kissing her intimately and she wasn't screaming blue murder, wasn't struggling like a wronged woman. He was, somehow, melting her resistance, wearing away her anger and frustration, causing many, many unexplained emotions to rise to the surface...

Why did she feel this compulsion to reach up and wind her arms around his neck, press her body close against his? Why did her mouth want to part a little more, accept the dominance of his kiss? Had she learnt nothing about herself?

When finally he released her, Christy found that she could barely stand, was shaking all over. She wasn't sure what to do, where to look, how to behave.

It had been three years since she had felt like that.

'Let's start over, shall we, Christy?' His voice was deep, enticingly without scorn or amusement. That voice, those eyes, those lips...

It shocked her that just for a moment she even considered agreeing to his suggestion. Her body was reeling, her thoughts were flying off in all directions. It would have been so easy then to raise her eyes and slowly nod, to agree to a truce, to give in to the persuasive charm that could be turned on and off like a tap.

But easy wasn't Christy King's way.

'Drop dead!' she snapped, and without waiting for a reaction she picked up her beloved bag and marched briskly down the track.

CHAPTER FIVE

CHRISTY felt as if she had been walking for miles, hours, and still no change in the scenery. She glanced down at her watch and frowned disbelievingly. Just fifteen minutes had passed.

The pace she had set for herself was far too fast. She bit down on her bottom lip as the pain from her aching knee and the soreness at the back of her heels got progressively worse. Ignore it, she told herself; think of something else. These shoes for a start. They were much too good to walk over this uneven, dusty track, far too impractical. Over a hundred pounds of best Italian craftsmanship and design. She glanced fleetingly down at her feet and heaved a despondent sigh, cursing herself for not packing something sensible.

'Christy!'

She wanted to glance back, to see how far behind Drew was, but stubbornness wouldn't allow her to do so, just as it wouldn't allow her to stop and have a much needed rest. She stepped up her pace a fraction and grimaced at the pain in her heels again.

'Christy!'

He wasn't far behind her now. She registered the insistent, commanding tone and resolutely kept up her speed. If he thought she would come running just because he had called he had another think coming! She was still fuming, absolutely beside herself with annoyance at having allowed Drew to drag her into his

arms, kiss her as if . . . well, as if she were his woman
or something. Oh, the audacity of the calculating, low-
down——!

'When I call your name I expect a response, is that
clear?' He stopped Christy in her tracks and swung
her around to face him. 'You're not going to last more
than a couple of miles if you carry on with this childish
behaviour! We walk together and we walk at my pace,
OK?'

Christy brought herself up to her full height and
stared pointedly down at the firm, strong fingers that
were gripping her arm, but he made no move to release her, so she glared into his face instead and put
every single ounce of haughtiness she could into her
expression. 'And what if I don't happen to want to
walk alongside you and at your pace?' she retorted
icily, registering the fact that he looked as cool and
as relaxed as when they had started out, as if he were
on no more than a pleasant picnic, while she already
felt like death warmed up: hot and sweaty and ready
to collapse at any minute—well, perhaps not quite as
bad as that, but pretty dreadful just the same. 'I am,
thank you, quite capable of judging my own speed,'
she continued, 'and as the very sight of you makes
my blood boil—— Will you remove your hand from
my arm, please?'

'We walk together if it means I have to tie you to
me, or carry you over my shoulders!' Drew informed
her fiercely.

'Look——'

'Stop arguing, woman, or so help me——'

'What?' Christy demanded angrily, violet eyes
blazing. 'What will you do?'

He jerked her body close against his own in one
swift movement and Christy cursed her mistake as she
felt the automatic response rise up in her again. The
tangle of physical awareness and sharp antagonism;
this weird sensation, this angry shock and excitement
that simultaneously filled every part of her body. She
waited, trembling slightly as his clear blue eyes pierced
hers.

'Do you really want to know?' His voice was rough,
husky. She could sense the anger behind the control,
knew that another kiss was what he had in mind and
shivered because of it.

'N-no!' Her voice was barely more than a whisper.
'L-let me go!'

'And if I do—are you going to start acting with
some sense?'

She swallowed and managed a shallow breath,
found herself nodding in the affirmative.

'Right, then.' He released her with a satisfied nod
and took a pace backwards. 'Now sit down on this
bank and take your shoes off.'

Christy frowned, hesitated and then, after following the line of Drew's gaze, lifted the bottom of
her trousers and, gasping in surprise at the blood-
soaked mess of her heels, did as she was told.

Drew slung his haversack off his shoulders and
rummaged around on bended knee for a couple of
seconds before producing the first-aid tin. 'You're sure
you haven't got something more suitable to walk in?'
he asked as he cut a couple of strips of plaster off a
reel. 'Nothing at all?'

Christy worked hard at not grimacing as he reached
forward and slowly eased off her slender cream court
shoes. 'No.'

'Hold this, will you? I'll just dip this cotton wool in the stream.' He handed Christy the first-aid tin and she watched dejectedly as Drew climbed down the small incline to crouch low over the gushing water that looked so refreshing and cool. Her heels were a mess and they were sure to get worse and they had travelled no distance at all. It was a disaster—*she* was a disaster.

'Look, I realise that I'm going to be a hindrance,' she murmured when Drew returned; 'we've only travelled a mile or so. It would be better, wouldn't it, if you left me here and went on by yourself?'

'Is that what you want?' Drew glanced up at her, his mouth showing a hint of derision. 'First hurdle arrived at and you're not even prepared to attempt to jump?'

'No. . . no, it's not that!' Christy retorted angrily. 'I simply thought——'

'We stay together and we walk at a sensible pace.' His hands were cool against her skin. Christy held her breath as the strong, tanned fingers cleaned her heels, pressed the plaster firmly on to the large blisters. He shook his head as he snapped the first-aid tin shut. 'Your feet are a mess and they're going to get worse. Here, give me your bag. Let me see what other footwear you've got—you must have something better than those shoes.'

Before Christy could stop him, Drew had picked the holdall up from beside her feet and was rummaging none too carefully around inside.

'Do you mind?' She tried unsuccessfully to retrieve it from him. 'Look, those happen to be my things and they're private!'

She might as well not have spoken. 'These will do,'
Drew murmured. 'At any rate they'll be much better
that those shoes you've been wearing. Come on!' He
leant forward and, taking Christy's hand, jerked her
upright. 'See what you think.'

'I think,' Christy fumed, 'you have gone mad. I
am not wearing slippers!'

Drew's lips twitched. 'Why not? They'll save your
heels and they have quite a thick sole on them.' His
mouth curled as he examined them. 'I have to agree
they don't quite go with the outfit but what the hell?
Why not go mad and lose a little of that boring
fashionable respectability?'

'I'll be OK the way I am.'

'No, you won't,' he insisted. 'Blisters are hell—
you'll slow us up. Have no fear, as soon as we come
to civilisation, you can change back——' His lips
curled. 'After all, it wouldn't be the thing to allow
someone to see Christy King in carpet slippers, would
it?'

'They're towelling mules, actually!' she snapped
indignantly.

'Oh, well,' he replied mockingly, 'that makes all
the difference, then, doesn't it?'

'That's it—make fun of me! Use every opportunity
you can to deride and sneer and mock!'

There was a moment of silence and then Drew
grabbed the holdall, zipped it back up again and held
it out to her, his eyes, his whole face suddenly showing
no hint of humour. 'OK, you want to end up crying
with pain, then go ahead, wear your damn shoes!'

'B-but——'

'Take it!' He thrust the holdall none too gently into
her arms. 'At least then you'll be able to say you

stayed well-dressed to the last—— So what if blood is saturating your ankles, if you're in agony?' He gave a short humourless laugh and stared up at the sky. 'Christy King still managed to keep up appearances even though she was on her last legs!'

Christy shook her head and frowned as she hung her head and stared down at the dusty ground. What was wrong with her all of a sudden? Why did she always have to say and do the wrong thing? 'Drew, I——'

'Do you know something, woman?' he snarled, cutting her dead. 'You sure have a weird sense of priorities! And I sure as hell am sick to death of battling with you over petty, inconsequential things!'

Christy bit down on her bottom lip and watched as he stormed away up the track. She felt like howling her eyes out in frustrated anger. He was right. The mules were a good idea, she should have thought of them herself, and he was only trying to help, to save her some unnecessary pain. She sighed and glanced down at her heels, rubbing at her hot, stinging eyes. Damn Drew Michaels for being right, for treating her as if she were a child!

But I'm acting like one, she thought honestly. I'm acting like a complete idiot! Why? Why? She wanted to sink on to the grassy bank and cry like a baby there and then, but she knew that wouldn't get her anywhere.

She took a deep breath and quickly thrust her bare feet into the soft towelling mules, finding to her surprise that they weren't as difficult to walk in as she had anticipated.

'I'm sorry about the fuss just now,' she murmured. He was lounging casually on a bank, evidently waiting for her to catch up with him, hands behind his head, soaking up the shafts of sun that appeared like an oasis of warmth through the swiftly moving clouds. 'It's just that——'

'You've had a soft life and now that things are getting tough you can't handle it!'

Christy's lips parted. Drew's words had been flung at her with a casualness that stung. 'Th—that's not true!' she flashed indignantly.

He raised a dark brow in query. 'Isn't it?'

Is that what he really thought—that she'd had everything handed to her on a plate? She shook her head disbelievingly as a swift catalogue of images, disjointed, out of sequence, flashed into Christy's mind.

There had been good moments, she supposed, but they were few and far between; the children's home had been too large, too impersonal, too uncaring. She looked at Drew, her mind back in the imposing Victorian building. Ten years in a place like that—an easy life?

'Not at all!' Christy gritted her teeth. 'Look, I've just apologised!' she added indignantly. 'You were trying to help and I *was* sorry——'

Drew's mouth formed a mocking smile. 'But not any more?'

'Damn right not any more!' Christy snapped. 'An easy life? What the hell do you know about anything?'

'Do I detect hidden depths in that statement, layers of Christy King that have yet to be uncovered, discovered? Is there more to the glamorous chat-show hostess than meets the eye?'

She glared down at him, the swift, sudden surge of angry adrenalin causing her to breathe hard. What game was he playing now? she wondered, flashing eyes at the mocking smile that told her he couldn't give a damn. Was he stirring her up deliberately, provoking her, just so he would get some kind of reaction? 'Tell me, Drew,' she questioned with icy precision, 'what sort of a childhood did you have? Cosy middle-class sort of existence, was it? Mummy and Daddy both professionals?'

He looked at her for a moment, a lazy, considered kind of gaze, and then he said, 'My father was a lord—as I'm sure you very well know.'

'So life was good, was it?' Christy enquired. 'You were loved, cherished, given everything you could possibly need?'

'I have no complaints,' he replied coolly. 'My parents travelled a great deal, but we—my sister and myself—were well looked after. So,' he added musingly, 'it seems I'm right in feeling there's a point to these questions. Is this my cue to ask how it was for you? Are you about to tell me you were sent to the workhouse at the age of seven or something?'

He was only joking, but in a peculiar way he had almost hit the mark—she had been just a little under that age when her mother had given up her struggle to hold on to her children and abandoned them all to the care of the state. Christy felt her cheeks redden. She hadn't meant this to go so far. Why had she brought up childhood, for heaven's sake? Hadn't it taken her all her adult life to put all that firmly behind her?

'I...I don't discuss my private life!' she murmured, picking up her holdall, spinning from him awkwardly to continue walking up the track.

'But you enjoy snooping about, poking your nose into other people's lives,' Drew commented, joining her. 'Why is yours suddenly out of bounds?'

She threw him a glance as he walked alongside her. Against her better judgement she observed the strong, well-shaped profile, the length and thickness of his dark lashes, and admitted that he was the most attractive, virile man she had ever set eyes on. 'It's my job,' she replied, fighting to keep her thoughts under control. 'And besides, guests are invited on to my show—it's up to them whether they accept or not. Prying and snooping doesn't come into it.'

'No?'

'No!' Her voice had risen noticeably. She couldn't help it. Even though she knew he was winding her up deliberately, she couldn't help taking the bait. He was so infuriating. So cool and arrogant.

'And when they're on your show, these poor devils—your guests—what about the questions you ask, the ones that intrude and go beyond the boundaries of decent privacy? It's a live show. They're nervous, taken by surprise—don't you ever feel guilty about pushing so hard, forcing them into a corner?'

'Not at all!' Christy paused then, considering the pointlessness of putting her case. After all, why should she care that he had such an obviously low opinion of her work? What did he know anyway? 'Look, I simply ask the questions I believe the viewing public would like to hear. And the guests know what they're letting themselves in for. I'm well-publicised for being straight and to the point—if they don't like it they shouldn't accept in the first place, should they? Anyway,' Christy added, her violet eyes narrowing with suspicion, 'how come you suddenly seem to be an expert on my shows?'

Drew cast her a sardonic glance and murmured drily, 'I was on once—remember?'

She averted her gaze from his face and stared ahead with stony determination. 'Oh, yes,' she murmured, with a vagueness that sounded, to her own ears at least, quite convincing. 'So you were.'

'And, since our interesting liaison all those years ago, I have from time to time watched a few of your shows when I've been in this country. That surprises you?' Drew murmured, dark brows raised.

'Frankly, yes,' Christy admitted stonily. 'I suppose you've been waiting for me to fall flat on my face or something!'

'But of course,' he murmured drily; 'why else would I tune in?'

Christy threw him a sharp puzzled glance. Why else indeed?

Silence. Just the sound of their footsteps on the dry mud track and the whisper of wind, rustling the trees that edged the bank of the river.

Was he thinking about that time? Christy wondered. Had he relived that brief interlude in the hotel room over and over again, examined parts of it months, years later the way she had done?

She cast another surreptitious glance sideways and read absolutely nothing in Drew's expression.

No, of course he hadn't.

I was such an easy lay, she thought. Damn! Damn! What a fool! It still made her angry no matter how many times she tried to put the whole awful affair down to experience.

'Did you say something?' Christy jerked herself back into the present and looked behind. Drew had stopped walking and was surveying her with an intrigued air.

'I said do you want to stop here for a moment and have a drink and a rest? It's a nice spot. You've been deep in thought,' he commented drily, as Christy, realising her legs were as heavy as lead, joined him beside a particularly pretty patch where the river splashed and gurgled over huge boulders, causing a torrent of fresh white foam to spurt into the air. 'I was starting to become concerned,' he added mockingly. 'I didn't realise you could keep quiet for such a length of time.'

'There's a lot you don't realise,' Christy replied with a deliberately sweet smile.

'For example?' Drew was rummaging in the haversack. Christy eyed it hopefully, praying that he would produce something to eat. He looked across at her with eyes that were searching. 'So tell me! What for example?'

She hesitated. The tone of Drew's voice seemed to have changed. Flippant before, now...well, sort of intense, deadly serious. She found herself meeting his gaze, felt a swift surge of sudden awareness at the proximity of him. Oh, she shouldn't have agreed to this trip, to the interview, to anything! It was so foolish.

With deliberate effort, she schooled her voice into sounding light. 'Well, I'm not the ambitious, money-grubbing celebrity-basher you so obviously take me for!'

'I wasn't aware that was how I had described you,' Drew replied, steadily gazing into her eyes.

'Oh, not in so many words,' Christy agreed drily, 'but one thing I do pride myself on is my intuitive abilities—I'm not stupid, I know what you think of me!'

'Intuition—ah, yes, a woman's special sixth sense.' He smiled lazily. 'And what is yours telling you now? Any insights into my soul, into what I might be thinking at this moment?'

She saw his eyes shift from her face, travel the length of her body in slow appraisal. Up and down, taking his time, a sensual smile curving the corners of his mouth. Christy swallowed, burning beneath his gaze, feeling naked and vulnerable and ... she swallowed again ... and aroused by the burning intensity of his eyes. His gaze indicated lust, and although her head told her that it meant little or nothing to be wanted by someone who was as sexually active as Drew Michaels she still found herself affected physically by the messages that he was sending with so blatant a look.

'Do you know what I'm thinking, Christy, what I would like to do now?' His voice was low, husky, dripping sensuality.

She must not allow this to happen, she must not feel this way simply because Drew Michaels had deigned to look at her. Christy had stopped breathing. Suddenly she didn't feel in control any more. Waiting. Just waiting for him to make a move, to end this tormenting mixture of agony and ecstasy.

'I could touch you, Christy. Shall I? Shall I kiss you again? Would you like that?' He watched her and she quivered beneath his burning gaze. The stillness of his taut, dark features compelled her, mesmerised her, left her weak and powerless as a new-born kitten.

'Anticipate, Christy. Imagine. Remember how it feels when we're together, when we are touching one another, making love... You were very passionate, Christy, do you remember?' Drew's eyes glittered. '"Brief, unmeaning sex"—it hardly fell into that category, did it?'

'I don't want to talk about it,' Christy murmured. 'Please, Drew, stop this!' she added breathlessly, turning from him, fighting hard to recover her composure. But she could think of nothing else. Her violet eyes were wide, unblinking, as she watched his slow, lazy smile. The need that had lain dormant for so long was growing with every passing second and there was nothing she could do about it as she relived the intense pleasure of that time, those moments...

CHAPTER SIX

'YOU think I'm going to fall for this . . . this charm all over again?' Christy demanded shakily. 'You think I don't know why you've brought me here? You're such a calculating bastard! I wouldn't put it past you to have engineered that landing, just so you could put me through all this agony!'

'That statement's a little melodramatic, even for you,' Drew murmured, 'and I'm sorry to disappoint you, Christy, but not even I would endanger lives to prove some sort of point—whatever you believe that point to be.' He raised an enquiring brow. 'What am I supposed to be doing, by the way? Care to enlighten me?'

'Why did you want to be interviewed?' Christy demanded bluntly. 'And by me.'

'Aren't you the best there is?'

'That wasn't the question and you know it!' she flared. 'You hate interviews, you hate publicity——'

'Maybe I've changed,' he drawled infuriatingly, determinedly keeping cool and relaxed and in doing so managing to make Christy feel as if she was over-reacting. 'Let's just say I felt enough time had passed since my last sortie into the world of self-promotion. Let's just say I had an irresistible urge to see you again after all these years.'

'Damn you!' Christy scrambled to her feet and felt the unsteadiness of her limbs as she picked her way down to the water's edge. She couldn't believe she was allowing him to do this to her. Where was her self-esteem? For goodness' sake, had she forgotten her resolutions? Had she forgotten how much she hated him?

The water was icy cold, sharp like a knife against her skin. Christy stared down at her feet, at her shiny red toenails, and fought hard against the tears that were burning her eyes.

'Would you like something to eat? I have some biscuits and fruit here.'

She looked across to where he lounged beside the water and wished she could tell him what to do with his food, that she would choke on any morsel he offered, but she couldn't. She felt faint with hunger, desperate for anything just to get rid of the gnawing pain in her stomach.

He held out a packet of digestives and an orange. 'Not much else, I'm afraid. If you want a drink it will have to be the river.'

Christy licked at her dry lips and glanced at the gushing water. 'Is it clean?'

Drew shrugged. 'Looks OK. Not that we've got much choice anyway—it's that or die of thirst.'

'I can live in hope!' She came towards him, taking a handful of biscuits and the orange, careful to avoid his touch. 'Anything would be preferable to the agony of having to endure your company!'

The light was fading. She saw it and felt despair rise within. The track was still going strong, which was more than could be said for Christy.

She was losing faith in her ability to keep on going any longer. They had stopped for rests on a couple of occasions with Christy pointedly sitting apart, pointedly ignoring him, but she still felt utterly exhausted, utterly spent.

What would they do if nothing turned up? What would *she* do? The prospect of having to sleep out here in the wilderness had just never occurred to her, or, if it had, she had patently refused to think about it. Now, as moths and bats began to make their nightly expeditions all around, it became something of a reality and it horrified her.

'This looks reasonable.'

She stopped, turning at the sound of Drew's voice— they had hardly spoken more than a handful of words since that first rest by the water; now she watched in alarm as he threw the haversack on to the ground beneath a small clump of trees and began to remove things from it.

'What are you doing?'

He glanced up as she came towards him and shrugged. 'What does it look like? I'm setting up camp.'

'You're what?' Christy's voice was sharp with alarm. 'But... but we can't stop now. We've got to go on. The farm could be just around the corner.'

Drew threw her a deliberately patient look—the sort of expression that was reserved for someone who was quite, quite dim. 'I know exactly where the farm is, Christy, and it's too far for us to make it there tonight. I don't know whether you've noticed but it's getting dark. It's almost ten o'clock. We have to rest.'

'You... you mean sleep? Out here? Without a tent or anything? You're mad!' Her voice was rising with anxiety.

'So what do you propose?' Drew enquired tightly. 'That we carry on, blundering in the dark? We've been walking a long time, Christy; we can't go on forever. Apart from anything else it's not safe——'

'What do you mean it's not safe?' she asked frantically, cutting in with alarm, imagining all sorts of terrors—from bands of marauding strangers to beasts that roamed in the wilderness as soon as the hours of darkness fell.

'Will you stop this, Christy, and calm down?' Drew growled. 'Grasp hold of the situation and stop acting like an idiot. We cannot walk on in the dark! Now stop getting hysterical and come over here.'

'You *knew* we would have to spend the night out here, didn't you? You knew and yet you still insisted we walk!'

'Just think of it as a new experience, Christy,' Drew instructed smoothly. 'Now it's a warm evening so we shouldn't have too much trouble with the cold, but even so you should look through your precious bag and find as many things as you can to put on,' he told her. 'Just layer it over what you're wearing. I brought a tarpaulin from the plane, just in case this eventuality arose——'

'Why didn't you tell me about this?' Christy demanded.

He gave a careless shrug. 'What would have been the point? You would only have made a fuss similar to the one you're making now. It wasn't worth the hassle.' He reached into the haversack and pulled out a light rug, the sort that was used for picnics. 'There's this too.' He glanced up and saw Christy's furrowed brow. 'Don't look so worried. We might be a bit cold, but we won't die of frostbite—not in late June at any rate.'

It's not the prospect of getting cold that's worrying me, Christy thought wildly.

'You expect me to share those with you?'

It wasn't true, was it? She had to lie beside him? He honestly expected her to spend the whole night cuddling beneath the blankets next to him as if it were the most normal thing in the world?

'You have a better idea?' The terseness of his voice clearly told her he wasn't in any mood for an argument.

Christy threw him a frosty look and, picking up her holdall, turned smartly on her heel.

'Where exactly do you think you're going?' Drew's voice was coldly mocking in the fading light.

'I don't know,' Christy shouted, 'and I don't care! All I know is I do not want to spend the night here with you!'

He didn't run after her. Had she expected him to? No! she told herself swiftly. No, of course not!

Her feet were aching. She strode for maybe twenty metres in a sort of angry trance. She wasn't sure what she was doing, where she was going any more. The whole dreadful day had been so much of a strain, so dreadfully tiring that all of a sudden she couldn't even think straight. I've lost my senses, she thought, as she stumbled clumsily into a boulder and gave a little cry of pain. What do I think I'm doing?

Suddenly he was there beside her, taking her hand, removing the heavy holdall from her grasp. 'Come on, Christy, the spot I've selected is much nicer.' His voice was firm and insistent with just an edge of sympathy to it. Curiously the sound of it made her suddenly want to weep.

She let him guide her safely back to the place beneath the trees and felt the slow, insidious trickle of warm tears on her cheeks.

'OK. So you've brought this bag a long way and I never thought you'd do it,' Drew remarked. 'But have you got anything that is the slightest bit of use inside? Because now is the time to produce it. Something warm maybe; jumpers, socks, that sort of thing?'

Suddenly Christy felt almost too weary to talk. She flopped down on the dry grass and shook her head silently, glad that in the dusky light Drew wouldn't be able to see the tears rolling down her cheeks. 'Just the cardigan I was wearing earlier, some stockings, nothing else that's much use—not for out here in this wilderness at any rate,' she murmured, picturing her selection of impractical designer-label outfits.

Drew's expression showed no surprise. 'Well, I have my jumper; you can put this on.' He dragged the garment from around his waist and before Christy knew what was happening he was drawing it over her head, dressing her as if she were a little girl. 'Better?' She nodded mutely. 'Are you hungry? Would you like some more biscuits or an apple? It's all we have left, I'm afraid.'

'No.' Christy surreptitiously brought up a hand to wipe away the sheen of wetness from her face. 'No, thank you.' She hesitated and then added, 'But I would like to...you know...' She blushed like crazy in the darkness.

'Use the bathroom?' Drew's voice betrayed amusement. 'Well, take your pick, Christy.' He indicated the valley with a sweep of his arm. 'There's plenty of space. I promise I won't look.'

Afterwards she rinsed her hands in the stream, freshened herself by splashing cool water over her face. When she got back she opened her bag and pulled out a towel and a toothbrush, suddenly immensely glad that she had lugged her belongings with her, despite the fact that Drew thought she was mad and her arms felt twice as long as when she had set out. In the morning, she promised herself, she would find a quiet spot and wash and change her clothes, but for now this much would have to do.

'I'm just going to go down to the stream to brush my teeth.'

'OK. Fine. Just don't go wandering off in the wrong direction, will you? I don't fancy the prospect of searching for you in the pitch-dark.

'Feel better?' he asked a few minutes later.

Christy paused in her task of brushing her long, long hair and threw him a brief nod. He was already stretched out, lying on his side, with his head propped up on one elbow. She knelt on the ground beside him and replaced her things in the bag, aware that he was watching her with that particular expression that never failed to make her feel acutely vulnerable and aware of him. 'Would . . . would you like the use of my towel and toothpaste?'

'Thanks, but no, thanks,' he drawled. 'In the morning maybe, but not now. I really would like to get some sleep.' He reached out a hand. 'No, don't put the towel away. Look, if you fold it up you can use it for a pillow. Come on.' He patted the tarpaulin that he lay on. 'There's no need to look so unlike the Christy King I've become accustomed to—I won't bite, I promise.'

Christy wasn't quite sure why she offered him the use of her things—she shouldn't have, not after the way he had treated her earlier. She cursed silently, annoyed with herself for not sustaining the cold, hard image. It was so difficult, though. She was tired, and deep down extremely upset at having crashed, at having no control over the current position she found herself in. Damn! She had promised herself that she would be better prepared this time and now here she was about to spend a whole night with Drew in this most vulnerable of situations.

Slowly she zipped up the holdall and then, after folding the thick fluffy towel into a square, lay reluctantly down beside Drew. Without a word he placed the blanket over her and then moved on to his back and closed his eyes.

It was quite an anticlimax—not that she had wanted anything else, she reminded herself swiftly, but she had expected something—some sort of quip, a few derisive remarks before he settled down for the night. She lay on her back and stared up at the sky feeling dreadfully exposed, dreadfully nervous. She scanned her memory for times when she had gone camping before and decided this was the first, and, if she had any say in the matter, last occasion. Drew, it seemed, took to this outdoor stuff like a duck to water, but not her. She craved the luxury of a hot, soapy bath, the comfort of her own large four-poster bed.

Had Drew really dozed off? She turned her head, glancing in his direction, and listened to the tell-tale rhythmic sound of his breathing. The night loomed ahead long and lonely. She wished with all her heart that she were asleep too; obliterating what remained of this harrowing day would be bliss.

There were a few stars visible now in the deepening dusky blue of the sky. Christy watched them for a long time, thought of all that had happened and then, after making sure she was at the very edge of the tarpaulin, promptly fell fast asleep.

She awoke some time later while it was still very dark. She stared into the inky blackness and listened for a moment, trying to decide what had woken her, and then she sat upright. There were many sounds and all of them seemed eerie and unnatural now that night had fallen. She stiffened at a rustling somewhere behind her, a high-pitched cry. Just an owl, she told herself firmly. Don't be so silly; it's nothing to worry about.

Then, when she had managed to convince herself that she should lie back down and try to get some more sleep, something light and soft fluttered across her face at speed, brushing against her skin, touching the strands of golden hair, moving them slightly as if they were in a breeze. Christy's reaction was humiliatingly predictable.

She screamed.

Drew jerked upright in the darkness beside her. A furiously muttered expletive then, 'Christy? What the hell's the matter? Are you all right?' His voice was deep and reassuringly urgent in the blackness. Christy couldn't see his face, but she could imagine the alert expression, rely on the superior physique beside her.

Thank heaven he's with me. The surprising thought flew unbidden into her mind and she corrected it swiftly. I'm not alone, she added; that's what I mean.

She was shaking a little, but she forced herself to sound reasonable and calm. 'It's...it's OK,' she murmured hastily. 'I didn't mean to scream. I...I think it was just a...a bat. It flew sort of close.'

'Look, where the hell are you? Are you actually on this tarpaulin or not?' Drew reached across, his hands searching her out, finally coming to rest on her lower back, at the place where the cascade of honey-coloured hair ended.

Christy stiffened at his touch and twisted awkwardly away. Why did his hands feel like fire when they touched her? Why did the briefest contact send the most outrageous signals shooting through every part of her body?

'What are you doing now?' he enquired as she stood up, hugging her arms around her body in the chill night air. 'Christy!'

Her eyes were more used to the overwhelming darkness now. She could make out Drew's rugged outline, knew, despite not being able to identify his expression, that he was exasperated with her. 'I won't be able to get back to sleep. I can't!' she insisted, running her hands almost frantically through her hair. 'All this nature, all these creatures that I can't see, creeping and crawling around.' She shivered a little and her voice trembled. 'And I'm cold. My back aches from the hard ground——'

'Come here!'

Christy inhaled a huge lungful of night air and struggled frantically with herself. She could feel panic rising to the surface. Drew gave her a second and then repeated his order—this time there was no mistaking the crisp tone of command. 'Stop getting yourself worked up, Christy, and do as I say! You can't stand there all night. It won't be light for...' he paused and she guessed he was looking at the luminous dial of his watch '...for another four hours—it's only just past midnight for goodness' sakes. You've...we've barely been asleep for a couple of hours.'

'I don't want to go to sleep!' Christy replied insistently. 'It's horrible lying out like this, all exposed and...'

'And what?'

Her voice had trailed away because she had been about to say frightened. It was weak and ridiculous, but she really felt uneasy out here in the dark. At home, even now, she still had a little light from somewhere when she slept; twenty-six and she was still behaving like a small girl, she thought; it seemed pathetic suddenly. 'I...I just don't like this,' she added, striving to keep the tremor from her voice.

'And you think I do?' His voice was low and even. 'But it's happened; we have to spend the night somewhere. Now come back over here and try again. There's nothing out here that will harm you, believe me.'

Isn't there? Christy thought wearily, eyeing his dark, solid outline as she lay back down and pulled the blanket up around her body.

'What are you doing?' Her voice was as sharp as a razor as Drew's arm pulled her towards him.

'Now don't get uptight! You're cold; if we lie closer together it will help get you warmer.'

Christy pushed his arm away decisively. 'And you expect me to believe that?' she asked incredulously. 'Come off it, Drew, I wasn't born yesterday!'

She heard him expel an impatient sigh. 'Do you really think I'd try it on out here, woman?' He sounded suddenly bored, as if the thought were totally ridiculous. 'Do give me credit for some finesse,

Christy.' He withdrew his arm and she felt his movement next to her and then the whole of his rugged length was close against her body, not in a way that had any hint of seduction, though, she acceded—or at least not intentional seduction anyway—but it was there, close and exuding male potency, reminding her, driving her wild . . .

Christy held her breath and fought hard with herself. The nerve-endings along every inch of her body were tingling with wild, erratic abandon at the merest hint of his touch. She hated herself in that moment, for being so weak, for allowing herself to succumb to such blatant physical needs; her own inadequacies.

'Relax, Christy.' His whispered words were warm against her neck. 'Lie still and use your common sense. You have my solemn word that I won't lay a finger on you.'

'And am I supposed to be reassured by that useless statement?' she enquired with an agreeable amount of waspishness in her voice. 'You can't honestly believe——'

'Listen, woman! Are you feeling warmer or not?'

'A . . . a little.'

'Well, then,' Drew rasped, 'stop quibbling and go to sleep. We have probably got a very long day ahead of us tomorrow and you're going to need all the rest you can get.'

Dawn was beginning to break when Christy woke and found herself snuggled warmly into the protective curve of Drew's body. She lay still, aware of his arm heavy about her waist, of his body pressed up close against her back, and tried not to breathe too conspicuously lest she should wake him. What was she doing like this? Even closer. Even more wrapped up in his arms than before. Hadn't her last waking thought been to extricate herself deftly from Drew at the earliest possible moment?

She released a little sigh and shifted slightly. One of his legs was trapping her own. She tried to move but found it was impossibly heavy.

'You want me to move? Why not say so?'

His voice was a sleepy whisper against her ear. For a split-second Christy felt a sharp jagged edge of something approaching regret tear through her, a tangled mixture of images she didn't wish to examine too closely. What must it be like to wake up every morning in the embrace of a man such as Drew; to feel protected, cocooned in solid strength that somehow could hold with a gentleness that thrilled and surprised . . . ?

'I want you to move.' Christy breathed the words and waited. 'Did you hear what I said, Drew? Let me get up.'

Nothing.

'Drew, stop this—I'm warning you!' she tried not to sound desperate. She didn't want to be transparent, to allow Drew to see what sort of effect his close, close proximity was having on her, but it wasn't easy.

'It's too early, Christy,' he growled. 'Go back to sleep.'

Was he kidding? Christy thought wildly. Sleep? Now? With his body so close? She took a steadying breath and swallowed. 'If you don't move away by the time I've counted to three I'll—— '

'What?'

He had moved. Christy felt a swift surge of satisfaction, which was followed closely by dismay and then something approaching panic. 'What will you do? Tell me, Christy—I'm intrigued.'

He was above her, pinning her arms on either side above her head, staring down with a glint in the steely blue eyes that just blazed sensuality. Christy felt the sharp pain of desire, intermingled with wild anger, and knew in that moment that she would probably never have the sense to learn her lesson. 'Stop this, Drew. It's not the least bit amusing!' Her voice, at any rate, wasn't letting her down so badly; there was enough ice dripping off each syllable to cause frostbite.

'Do you see me laughing?'

No, she thought, staring up into the angular face, noticing for the first time the dark swarthiness around his jawline which only succeeded in making him look more rugged, more male. No! Her eyes shifted from the face to the strong column of his throat, back up to his stunning eyes that stared down at her unflinchingly. No.

'You haven't told me.'

'What?' Her voice was barely a whisper.

'What it was you were going to do, had I not moved?'

Christy pursed her lips angrily. 'Scream, I suppose.'

'You've never struck me before as the screaming type. Quite a tough little cookie, I had always thought.' Drew's lips twisted with amusement. 'Of course I know better now. Underneath all the glamour and ice-cool professionalism, there's quite a softie waiting to get out, isn't there? Tell me, Christy, how did the image come about? Was it something you decided on from the beginning, or did it evolve as a self-defence mechanism against the hard-nosed world of television?'

'This is very boring, Drew. Would you mind if I got up now?' It took a whole lot of composure to utter the words with just the right amount of disdain, but she succeeded—just. She managed somehow to control her body language, her expression, managed to deceive him into believing that she wasn't the least bit affected by his actions or his words.

'Yes, I would. You know, you really must get used to the fact that not everyone jumps when you say, Christy,' he drawled. 'You'll find that some people take exception to being continually ordered around.'

'Like you?'

'Especially me. In my world,' he added with a twist of his lips, 'women have a place and they stay there.'

Christy inhaled a furious breath. 'Typical!' she snapped. 'Just typical that on top of everything else you should be a raging chauvinistic swine!'

'Me?' Drew affected a hurt expression. 'How can you say that when it's well-known that I wholeheartedly approve of women pursuing a career? As long as they don't end up treading on male toes, of course,' he added with a quirk of amusement.

'Well, you hardly approve of me, then,' Christy retorted, 'because I seem to do that all of the time!'

'You've had to work hard, haven't you, Christy, since our very first meeting?' Drew remarked mockingly. 'Three years and just look at you now! A very successful, respected television journalist. Who would have thought it?'

Take 4 Love on call

Mills & Boon Love on Call romances capture all the excitement and emotion of a busy medical world... A world, however, where love and romance are never far away.

We will send you four LOVE ON CALL ROMANCES absolutely FREE plus a cuddly teddy bear and a mystery gift, as your introduction to this superb series.

At the same time we'll reserve a subscription for you to our Reader Service.

Every month you could receive the four latest Love on Call romances delivered direct to your door postage and packing FREE, plus a free Newsletter packed with competitions, author news and much more.

And remember there's no obligation, you may cancel or suspend your subscription at any time. So you've nothing to lose and a world of romance to gain!

FILL IN THE FREE BOOKS COUPON OVERLEAF

Your Free Gifts!

Return this card, and we'll send you a lovely little soft brown bear together with a mystery gift... So don't delay!

FREE BOOKS COUPON

YES Please send me four FREE Love on Call romances together with my teddy bear and mystery gift. Please also reserve a special Reader Service subscription for me. If I decide to subscribe, I will receive four brand new books for just £7.20 each month, postage and packing free. If however, I decide not to subscribe, I shall write to you within 10 days. The free books and gifts will be mine to keep in anycase. I understand that I am under no obligation - I may cancel or suspend my subscription at any time simply by writing to you. I am over 18 years of age.

EXTRA BONUS

We all love mysteries, so as well as the FREE books and Teddy, here's an intriguing gift especially for you. No clues - send off today!

9A4D

Ms/Mrs/Miss/Mr _____

Address _____

_____

_____

Postcode _____ Signature _____

One per household. Offer expires 31st March 1995. The right is reserved to refuse an application and change the terms of this offer. Offer not available for current subscribers to Love on Call. Offer valid in UK and Eire only. Readers overseas please send for details. Southern Africa write to IBS Private Bag, Randburg 2125. You may be mailed with offers from other reputable companies as a result of this application if you would prefer not to share in this opportunity please tick box ☐

Mills & Boon Reader Service
FREEPOST
P.O. Box 236
Croydon
CR9 9EL

SEND NO MONEY NOW

'Well, certainly not you for a start!' she retorted. 'I was just another empty-headed bimbo to you, wasn't I?'

'At first maybe yes,' he conceded without the least hint of embarrassment, 'but later—well, *I've* enjoyed watching your progress, watching you grow up on screen. It's been quite an illuminating experience over the years!'

'Are you saying that you have now revised your first impressions!' Christy enquired.

There was a slight pause. 'Possibly.' His expression was serious but his blue eyes clearly taunted.

'And am I supposed to feel flattered by this fact?' she asked stiffly, fighting hard to continue with the ice in her voice. 'Am I supposed to even care?'

'You can please yourself,' Drew remarked smoothly, 'as you usually do.'

He released her suddenly and as he did so she saw, just for a second, a glittering in his eyes, a certain tautness around his mouth, which for some curious reason had her experiencing regret. Perhaps she had misread him and that time...perhaps... No! She shook her head angrily as she scrambled to her feet. Of course she hadn't. She wasn't a fool. He was just playing another one of his games.

It was a new experience walking all alone with nature at this time of the morning. Christy made herself take deep breaths, made herself think of other things, mundane affairs that oozed normality.

She skirted the river for a while, clutching a change of clothes, her towel and sponge-bag, wondering if she dared risk a plunge—a very quick one, in the icy water. The shock would probably kill her, but surely

it would be better than how she felt now, grubby and
hot and extremely flustered? Besides, the cold water
might have a very good effect on her; it might, if she
were lucky, bring her to her senses, stop this continual
obsession with Drew. And then of course pigs might
fly.

She chose carefully, constantly glancing back,
making sure that there was no way Drew could see,
that anyone could see. Satisfied at last, Christy bent
down, carefully arranged her things on the bank clear
of the water and then hurriedly pulled off all her
clothes. This section which she had chosen was quite
a find—like an outdoor jacuzzi, she thought. A place
well-screened by trees, with easy access from the bank
to where the water rushed and flowed on its journey
towards the sea.

It was freezing. But she had expected that, steeled
herself for the agony of ice on her smooth golden skin.
She plunged in quickly, dropping to her knees, im-
mersing herself before the shock of the cold changed
her mind. It was glorious in a masochistic sort of way,
she reflected, gasping aloud. Quite, quite delightful
to feel cool and clean again.

Christy clutched hold of her body shampoo and
squeezed a good blob of it on to her hair, worked it
to a lather and then stood up a little and smoothed
some over her breasts and stomach. Her anxiety that
Drew might appear at any minute was beginning to
ebb away. The water had a stimulating effect; she felt
curiously uncaring suddenly at her unusually daring
exposure. So what if he sees me? she thought. So
what? We've made love. He knows more about my
body than any man alive. Even so, she found herself

washing quickly, ducking beneath the water to rinse herself as soon as she could.

The sun was beginning to feel quite warm. It was, Christy estimated as she lay on her back easing the bubbles from her hair, going to be a very hot day. Not a cloud in the sky even at this early hour.

'Need anyone to scrub your back?'

He was standing on the bank, leaning nonchalantly against the trunk of a tree, surveying her with eyes that just sparkled with amusement.

Christy rose up out of the water a fraction and then with every ounce of will she possessed she forced herself to relax back. Her first, almost overwhelming reaction to the sound of his deep resounding voice had been to jump up in alarm, dive for cover anywhere, anyhow; it would have been a futile gesture, of course, because there was nowhere for her to go, not without being well and truly seen by Drew. She was in full view of his gleaming male gaze and an inbuilt tendency towards modesty was strong within her. But something, perhaps an irritation because that was exactly what he expected her to do, what he wanted, made her fight the instinct for all she was worth. With her heart pumping wildly, she continued to lie in the gushing water with her head tipped back, continued to rinse her long, long hair. 'Thank you, but I'm already clean,' she called out calmly. 'I was just about to get out.'

It was a mistake saying that, of course, because now Drew was bending and holding out her towel, daring her to get up out of the water and walk towards him.

She cursed herself for being so foolish. She hesitated under cover of smoothing back her hair from her face and considered frantically. She had gone this far, had played the game admirably up to now; she couldn't duck out at this final hurdle, could she? If she hesitated now he would detect her embarrassment in an instant. He would revel in her discomfort.

Slowly she rose, the water streaming from her body, a thousand tiny rivulets of water traversing the slim, lithe frame, dripping from every part of her, and then she began picking her way over the rocks and the shingle bed of the river to the bank.

He was watching her. She risked a swift glance and saw the way Drew's eyes burned into her naked body, scorching her with their intensity. It was a moment she would never forget, a moment of sublime power. She possessed a body that many women envied, numerous men adored, yet she had always been a little self-conscious of it, a little afraid of its ability to attract. Now, as she waded through the water, she felt a kind of release, a curious power that sent shivers of erotic sensation spiralling through her body.

She raised her head, tilting her chin defiantly as she met his searing gaze and held out her hand for the towel. He handed it to her without a word, but not before his eyes had slowly and sensually traversed every inch of her skin, lingering deliberately on her full breasts, her slim thighs, her shapely legs.

Oh, how she wanted to grasp the towel and just run. Christy felt herself burning with the most intense embarrassment, but she would not, oh, no, she would not let him see that, allow him to take control of the situation.

'You like spying on people?' She had considered being more provocative with a comment such as, You seem to like what you see, something along those lines, a throw-away remark that would prove she wasn't the least bit affected by his appearance, but Christy credited herself with more sense than that. And anyway she wasn't sure if she could pull something like that off, or risk facing the consequences—she was pushing the boundaries of daring as it was; didn't she know better than anyone that it would be just like inviting trouble?

She wrapped the huge bath-sheet around her and added pointedly, 'I did want a private bath.'

'Not such an easy thing to acquire out in the open,' Drew replied. 'You should have warned me you were planning on bathing naked. I would have joined you. Actually,' he continued, his mouth curving as a hot, indignant flush rose to cover Christy's face, 'I wondered where you'd got to—you've been gone rather a long time.'

'Well, you've found me, haven't you?' Christy snapped, irritated by Drew's consistent ability to appear unfazed at all times. 'What was it you wanted?'

'Just to tell you that I think we should get started. I've packed up our sleeping things and brought your holdall for you.' He placed it on to the ground at her feet. 'Would you like some help to get dressed? I'm very deft with my hands! But then you know that, don't you?'

'I'm quite capable of dressing myself!' Christy snapped, trying her hardest to ignore the taunt. 'But I'd like some privacy; is that too much to ask?'

'Not at all.' Drew's mouth curled. 'I'll wait over here, but don't take all day. Five minutes at the most.'

Christy bent her head and began squeezing the water from her hair, relieved that he at least had the decency to look away. She held up the outfit she had chosen to wear and realised her hands were trembling a little. Keep cool, she told herself; don't let him get to you.

With a little sigh she dried herself and slipped on the dress. Such a shame, such a downright waste to put it on when all she was going to do in it was walk and walk out here, she thought. One of her favourite outfits too, a simple but elegant pastel pink shift dress cut like a dream that would undoubtedly be ruined somewhere along the way.

She glanced instinctively across to wear Drew lazed, as she struggled with the zip that she knew couldn't be done up without help. He was lazing against the trunk of a tree with his back towards her. Dared she ask him to help her? She considered swiftly, decided and before she could change her mind went across.

'Would you zip me up, please? I can't quite reach.'

Drew got to his feet and without a word took a hold of the zip.

She had known his touch would have a detrimental effect on her composure. She had guessed the slightest graze of his hands would feel like fire against the bare skin of her back, yet still the intensity of feeling, the surge of awareness, took her by surprise. She still, despite everything, persisted in underestimating the effect Drew Michaels had on her. Was he taking his time deliberately now just to remind her of that fact, or had the zip really stuck? Christy battled against the desire to jerk away and waited impatiently, every nerve-end taut and expectant as his fingers continued to brush against her skin.

'That's it.'

'I—thank you,' Christy breathed automatically.

'All set, then?'

'No, not just yet. I want to put on a little make-up.'

'You're kidding?'

Christy turned to face him, read the look of incredulity in his face and hesitated a fraction. 'N-no.'

'But what on earth for, woman? You're walking in the remote Scottish countryside, not taking a jaunt through Knightsbridge.'

Christy gripped her make-up bag more firmly. 'I just want to make myself look a little better, feel a little better. It won't take more than a couple of—— Hey! What the hell do you think you're doing?'

Drew had removed the bag from her hands and with one swift movement was hurling it far out into the flowing water of the river. 'No ridiculous make-up,' he growled. 'Now let's get on!'

She stared first at the water, at the brightly coloured bag that bobbed along for a little way before becoming lost in the swirling foam and then turned and glared with hatred at Drew. 'How could you? How could you do that?'

He threw her a bored look and gave a little shrug. 'It was just make-up, Christy; look upon it as a service, as a release. You know you look a hundred times better without all that muck on your face anyway.'

'Well, I happen to think otherwise! And besides,' Christy snapped wildly, 'that's not the point.' She pursed her lips together and shook her head in absolute fury. 'Are you listening to me?' she yelled after him.

He had begun walking, the haversack thrown nonchalantly over his shoulder. Drew wasn't taking a blind bit of notice. He really couldn't care less.

CHAPTER SEVEN

'So YE want t'use me car, d'yee?'

They had found civilisation—well, almost. It wasn't Christy's idea of paradise—one crumbling old shack that looked as if it was going to fall down any minute, a messy, unkempt front yard that didn't look in the least bit like her idea of a farm—but it was better than nothing. Even now, despite the evidence before her very eyes, she could scarcely believe they had reached the farm. She had felt desperate for all of the morning, convinced that the two of them were going round and round in circles.

She smiled her most charming smile now and willed the aged, weather-beaten man to agree.

Drew thrust his hand into the back pocket of his jeans and pulled out a wad of notes. 'We'll pay, of course,' he replied smoothly, 'and I'll leave my watch with you as collateral.'

The old man looked suspicious, so Drew deftly undid the clasp and held it out for examination. Roughly eight thousand pounds, Christy estimated, as she eyed the Rolex; a quality timepiece that might, or might not convince the old man to trust them. She watched as it was inspected and glanced despairingly at the battered old Ford Cortina that they would hopefully get in exchange. If the farmer had any sense, she thought, he'd keep the watch and pray they didn't return with the car at all.

'So how much would you want?' An edge of impatience was creeping into Drew's voice as the old man slowly turned the watch over in his grubby calloused hands. It was mid-morning; they had already been walking for six hours. 'One hundred, two hundred pounds?'

'Aye, that'll do.' The man swiftly took the money from Drew's outstretched hand. 'I'll get you the keys.'

'Do you think it will go?' Christy looked at the rust and the decidedly revolting interior and tried not to grimace as she got in beside Drew.

He turned the key in the ignition and threw her a savage look that spoke volumes. 'It'd better!'

It did, surprisingly well in fact. After a couple of miles of watching anxiously, of sitting rigid on the torn, plastic seat, Christy finally gave way to her tiredness, her almost overwhelming fatigue, and began to relax a little. She was so tired. Watching the monotony of the twisting narrow roads was having a hypnotic effect. Her eyes closed little by little, despite her resolution to keep awake, and after about ten miles of overwhelming relief at the fact that she was finally going home she slept.

When Drew touched her gently on the arm, she jumped a mile.

'We're here.'

Christy yawned and stretched like a cat. 'The airport already?' She gave a little sigh. 'That was good going.'

Not the airport. When she opened her violet eyes wide and looked ahead through the smeary windscreen, she wondered why she had ever imagined Drew would do the decent thing and tell the truth.

She got out without a word and slammed the car door shut. He had walked on ahead, was inserting a key into the solid-oak door of the farmhouse.

'I would be grateful if you would give me the keys to the Cortina.' Christy held out her hand and felt pride at the calmness of her voice. 'Stupid of me to believe what you said about the airport——'

He turned and threw her a vaguely puzzled look. 'Airport? I don't believe I mentioned anything about an airport.'

Hadn't he? Christy hesitated, frowning slightly, struggling to recall with a brain that felt inadequate. No, she thought, perhaps he hadn't... She straightened up and pursed her lips with anger. 'Well, I talked about the airport, then, but you mentioned home. You led me to believe we would go straight back. To London,' she added pointedly. 'That is where I live——'

'And I here.' Drew arched a dark brow. 'Come on, Christy, let's get inside first——' He looked tired; clearly an argument was the last thing he desired.

'I want to go back to London!' She felt the sting of tears suddenly and realised with dismay that she was shaking like a petulant child. She couldn't face another few hours of Drew's company. She wouldn't! It would be too much, on top of everything that had gone before. 'I would like the keys. Give them to me, please.'

'No.' His voice was quiet and firm. 'You are in no fit state to drive. Come on. Inside!'

She couldn't believe he was doing this to her. After all that she had been through. Christy planted her feet firmly on the ground and continued to hold out her hand. 'I want the keys. Hey!' Her voice rose an octave. 'What are you doing?'

She knew very well what he was doing, but it didn't stop her asking the question. With one swift movement he had walked forward, picked her up and was now proceeding to carry her inside. 'This is ridiculous,' Christy gasped, struggling a little in his arms. 'Put me down at once!'

'No, I will not!' Drew growled. 'You're coming inside.'

'You cannot do this to me!' Christy ground out. 'I won't allow it!'

'I'm already doing it, Christy, so there's absolutely no point in getting worked up all over again,' he remarked with infuriating calm. He placed her gently on to her feet once they were inside and firmly shut the door. 'Well, we finally made it. Now, first things first. Would you like to freshen up while I prepare us some food?' He spoke casually, pleasantly as if the previous scene had never taken place, as if they had just arrived as planned to do the interview.

Christy glared. It was lost on him, of course, because the curtains were drawn, but it made her feel just a little better. 'You don't seem to be taking any notice of me, Drew. Why is that?' she asked. 'Can't your ego accept the fact that I don't want to spend another minute in your company—is that it? To be stranded in the remote Scottish Highlands with you might be some women's idea of fantasy, but it doesn't appeal to me in the slightest! I have just endured the most agonising twenty-four hours of my entire life; survived a storm and an unexpected landing, walked goodness knows how many miles, been driven in the

most disgusting vehicle and now, *now* you expect me
to want to stay here with you——'

'Want doesn't come into it.' Drew walked across to
the windows and opened them wide, began drawing
back the curtains, so that sunlight flooded the room.
'You're staying with me as agreed, whether you like
it or not.'

It took Christy a full thirty seconds to grasp the
situation. For another thirty, she stood and watched
as Drew moved purposefully around the room, and
refused to believe it. She swallowed and felt the blood
drain from her face. 'You're...you're kidnapping me?
Holding me prisoner? Is that what you're saying?'

Drew's mouth curved easily, proving what Christy
already suspected—that he wasn't the slightest bit
concerned by the fact that he had behaved . . . was behaving in this way, treating her like this. 'As usual
you have a rather melodramatic way of putting
things,' he murmured, 'but yes, if that's how you
choose to look at it, I am. But just for a little while
and purely for your own good.' He gazed at her with
a critical eye. 'Now don't look so down-hearted,
Christy. Just think of all the journalistic miles you'll
get out of this when you get back. I can just see it
now—'DREW HELD ME CAPTIVE!' or 'MY WEEK OF
TORMENT WITH DREW MICHAELS!' He smiled across
at her. 'It would have to be worth a few thousand in
the tabloids at the very least.'

'Money!' Christy spat the word in his face. 'Do
you honestly think I'd do something like that?' She
spun away, tried not to show him that she was concerned by what he said. Did he really think she was
that sort of person? Did he really think that she'd do
almost anything for money?

When he replied and she found relief flooding through her, she felt even more annoyed, more confused, because, she realised, it had mattered a great deal that he shouldn't think that badly of her...

'No, I don't. I was winding you up. Something...' He paused and Christy saw a flicker of a frown cross his face, an expression of puzzlement that surprised and intrigued her. 'Something that I seem to do, despite my better judgement.' He turned and glanced out of the huge picture window, looked towards the beautiful expanse of blue water that glittered in the sunlight. 'Besides,' he added drily, 'that sort of thing would tarnish the image, wouldn't it? Far too sordid for someone of your calibre.'

He was doing it again. Putting her down. 'You didn't really mean a week?' She turned back, was facing him with her features composed, her voice cool. She wouldn't let him do this to her, play these games. She had pride. She wouldn't let him hurt her so. 'Is that how long you plan to keep me here against my will?'

'Would you like it to be longer?' he drawled, raising a quizzical eyebrow. 'Sorry, Christy, but unfortunately I have schedules to keep——'

'And you think I don't?' she snapped furiously.

'I know you don't.'

'What?' Her eyes sparked with anger. 'How do you——?'

'Tut, tut. I can see you've underestimated me, Christy!' His voice was as mocking as his expression. 'You really should have learned not to do that. I checked with your personal assistant—what's her name? Elizabeth Fowler; she was most helpful. Gave me all the information I wanted.'

Christy felt faint with disbelief. This wasn't happening, was it? 'She... she had no right.'

'Oh, you mustn't blame her. She thought she was doing you a favour. I can be particularly persuasive when I want to be.' His mouth widened into a seductive smile. 'But then you of all people should remember that.'

'Is there...?' She hesitated a fraction, tried hard not to think about that night... their love-making... her body frantically entwined with his...
'Tell me, is there some point to all of this? Or have you just gone completely mad?'

Drew appeared to consider her question seriously for a moment. Then his mouth curved and he smiled what looked like the smile of a perfectly sane man. 'Maybe I have, maybe I haven't. It's hard, don't you think, to stand back and judge, view yourself as others see you? Let's just say I see this as a mission. I needed a break from the shallow world we both inhabit. So did you——'

'Am I supposed to understand what you're talking about?' Christy enquired, struggling to keep her composure intact.

Drew considered. 'At this stage no; that would be a little too much to expect.'

'Stop talking in riddles!' Christy yelled. 'Let me have the car keys, damn you!' She threw herself at him. A sudden, violent movement that clearly took Drew by surprise. For a moment she thought he was going to fall, and that she would go with him, crashing on to the hard, cold, quarry-tiled floor of the living-room, but his reflexes saved them both. Drew swung around, catching Christy's flailing arms as he did so, and held her close against his body. For a moment

she struggled as anger surged through her veins and
then suddenly the frustration and the energy seemed
to seep from her limbs and she was still in his arms,
sobbing as if her heart would break.

Drew held her for a very long time, waiting patiently, stroking back the strands of long hair, gently
rocking her back and forth in his arms while Christy
cried and cried and cried. She wasn't sure what was
happening any more. She didn't understand how she
could hate him so much and yet still find it
comfortable, right to sob in his arms as if she were a
little girl. He surely had brought her to this and yet
here she was allowing him to comfort her, to whisper
soothing words, to hold her. I'm a strong woman, she
thought, between sobs; I shouldn't be behaving like
this. No, I'm not, I'm a total mess. What is wrong
with me?

'Christy?'

That was another thing, she thought. Her name
shouldn't sound so wonderful on his lips. She
shouldn't allow herself to be fooled by the deep, magnetic tone that hinted at all kinds of things that could
never be true. He was an actor, after all; she had to
remember that.

'You need to rest.' He tilted her away from his body,
holding her at arm's length, surveying Christy's tear-
stained face with eyes that made her feel utterly
foolish, because they were totally without any hint of
emotion. 'Let me take you upstairs and show you to
your room. We have certain luxuries here—there's an
en suite bathroom. And a lock on the door,' he added
pointedly. 'You can relax, unwind while I make us
some lunch.'

She shouldn't trust him. She shouldn't be allowing him to lead the way up a quaint winding staircase. She shouldn't be so meek!

'Did you sleep well?'

Christy had slept like a log. She had flopped on to the neatly made cast-iron bed after her bath and entered the world of the unconscious the second her head had hit the pillow. She nodded, surprised that despite everything she should feel so refreshed now. 'Yes, I did, thank you.' She had decided on her approach upstairs, while dressing: cool and aloof. A haughty detachment that would surely make Drew see after some short time that this whole idea of his was utter madness.

'You look better anyway. And you've left the make-up off. A great improvement.'

Christy speared him with a look of pure ice, valiantly trying not to notice how good he looked with damp hair and a fresh change of clothes. 'I had no choice. You threw it away—remember?'

Drew's mouth curved. 'Oh, yes,' he murmured casually. 'So I did. And looking at you now I can see it was the right thing to do.' His eyes traversed the short powder-blue dress she was wearing, lingered deliberately on the embroidered bodice. 'Right, then. We'll eat. Outside, I think, beside the loch. It's a wonderful evening.'

Christy looked at him sharply. 'Evening?' she queried.

'That's right.' He glanced automatically down at his bare wrist and then turned to the digital reading on the built-in hob. 'Just past six. You slept a long time.' He picked up a tray and indicated a bottle of wine and some glasses that were waiting on a side-board in the kitchen. 'Bring those out, will you?'

It was an idyllic spot. Christy cast her gaze over the water, shading her eyes from the evening sun, and wished she could relax, enjoy it more. The farmhouse really must have been quite a find—if you relished total peace, total seclusion, that was. Nothing around for miles. Not even a phone. Just the craggy, robust building and a winding track that skirted away through some trees to join the real road at some point.

Where were the keys to the Ford Cortina? In Drew's pocket? Christy stared out at the loch and frantically tried to remember what he had done with them. She could find them—they had to be somewhere—take them when he wasn't looking, drive away. Oh, yes, that would show him!

'Come and eat, Christy! The food's getting cold.' She turned at the quiet, commanding tone of his voice and realised he was close behind her. Not touching, not intimidating, just close. Reading her thoughts. 'Escape is futile, Christy, you know that. The keys are in a safe place. You won't find them.'

'I was looking at the loch,' Christy replied evenly, 'It hadn't even crossed my mind.' She turned properly and faced him, managed somehow to school her expression, steady her voice. 'You seem intent on playing this ridiculous game, Drew. And, as you've already pointed out, I have nothing on for the next few days. I can be patient. You'll realise the mistake you're making sooner or later. I can wait. In the meantime I'll do my best to enjoy the scenery.'

He smiled then. Such an infuriating, knowing look, which had Christy almost losing her hard-fought-for composure. 'You think...!' She stopped herself, calmed her voice. 'You think,' she continued quietly, 'that you know me, don't you? That you can predict what I'll say, what I'll do. How I'll react to given situations——'

'Some of the time.' His voice was as quiet as her own. 'Oh, yes, definitely some of the time. Now, for instance——' his voice was husky suddenly '—if I move a little closer, touch the edge of your cheek very gently, very softly. You see?' He raised one lazy, dark brow as Christy shivered faintly. 'Instant reaction.'

She struggled—oh, how she struggled to hold her ground, not to let his touch, his closeness, his voice, his look have any effect on her. It wasn't fair, she thought. It simply wasn't right that her body should be so treacherous.

'Don't paw me!' She knocked his hand away. 'If you think I'm going to fall for your seduction skills all over again——!' She glared at him angrily.

'*Paw* you?' Drew's voice was even, seemingly calm, but there was a note of incredulity, a certain something in the inflexion that told Christy she had overstepped the mark. 'Oh, no! Never paw, Christy. Never that.' His eyes darkened perceptively, mirroring the deep azure of the loch beyond. 'Stroke,' he murmured, 'massage...graze...squeeze...lick...all of those things, but never anything so obtuse, so insensitive ...'

She had allowed him to come too close. Christy felt the stirring, deep in the very heart of her, as Drew placed a finger very lightly on to her trembling lips. Slowly, oh, so slowly, he traced the luscious outline, the soft pink fullness of her mouth, and then, as if in slow motion, he bent his head and kissed the place where his finger had rested.

Christy automatically felt herself respond as his mouth explored the quivering softness, as his tongue lazily invaded the warm, moist interior. On and on. Absolute command. She trembled as she fought against the growing desire. How she wanted to wind her arms around his neck, draw his body closer, press herself against the hard male length, return the kiss that was at this very moment causing her senses to crash into pieces around her.

If Drew hadn't pulled back in that next moment, Christy knew she would have lost any last vestige of pride; she knew with a humiliating certainty that she would have offered herself to him without condition. He, it seemed, also knew. 'In time,' he assured her, 'but not now. It's too soon, Christy, far too soon.'

She didn't understand what he meant. Didn't understand anything—least of all herself. With a look of complete animosity that somehow managed to conceal the despair she felt, Christy turned on her heel and went back inside the farmhouse.

She had slept too long that afternoon. Now, at past midnight, she felt curiously refreshed and wide awake. With a careful hand she shot back the bolt and lifted the latch of her bedroom door. The farmhouse was dark and silent. She had heard Drew come up to his room at just before eleven. He had to be asleep.

The stairs creaked loudly as she descended. She held her breath and waited, listened with every part of her for the sound of his bedroom door opening. Nothing. All quiet.

Moonlight streamed into the rooms downstairs, marking out Christy's path with its eerie, silvery light. She padded silently through the living-room into the kitchen and raided the cupboards for any food she could lay her hands on. She had missed the evening meal and now she was starving. When she had munched her way through half a crusty loaf, she wandered back through into the other room and stared thoughtfully out at the loch.

She couldn't stay here. She couldn't allow herself to be humiliated by Drew any longer. He was playing some sort of calculated game, tormenting her, dangling her at arm's length, letting her have some line, now reeling her in, like a strong-willed fisherman who fancied a little bit of fun, with an equally strong-willed but rather dim-witted fish.

She knew where the keys of the Ford Cortina were— or at least she hoped she did. He had slipped them into the pocket of his jeans before and she felt sure he would have transferred them to the clean ones he had put on while she had slept. It would be the most obvious thing—to keep them on his person, the surest means of making sure she didn't come across them. Christy nodded firmly. They would be upstairs—in his room. She swallowed and took a huge steadying breath. So, she would go upstairs and quietly open the door to his bedroom, she thought calmly, and then... She tried to imagine herself doing it. Tried to imagine herself being that brave...

His door opened easily. No creaky hinges, no squeaks. It was a good start. Christy felt a little better as she pushed the door open a fraction and very slowly, very cautiously stuck her head around. It was a fairly large room, basically furnished like her own with good-quality furniture, thick hand-woven rugs placed at strategic intervals on the polished wooden flooring. What little there was in the room was un-

doubtedly the best; after all, she reminded herself,
Drew Michaels was a millionaire many times over.

Her eyes swivelled to the bed and she held her breath
as the sight of him, clearly naked beneath the tousled
sheet that only half covered his torso. He was asleep,
she felt sure of it. But even so it took a full thirty
seconds before she dared to move forward into the
room. He looked magnificent in the moonlight.
Christy's gaze helplessly travelled the length of him,
surveying the broad, rugged frame, the contours of
glistening muscle that were defined more clearly than
ever before. He was laying face down, his firmly
muscled forearms sprawled on either side of the pillow.
She could see his profile turned towards her in relaxed
repose and felt the tremor of fear and excitement shoot
through every part of her as he moved in his sleep,
changed his position so that now he was lying on his
back, his arms flung above his head. She stiffened
and waited, her heart beating fit to burst, her brain
screaming that she was mad, totally mad to have risked
coming so close.

Why do I have to keep looking at him? Christy
closed her eyes for a moment in despair and then
opened them quickly again, following the line of dark
hair that began at the base of his throat, spread across
the pectoral muscles of his chest, on down over the
flat plane of his stomach, narrowing until it reached...
She spun away, sick with disgust at herself, feeling
like a voyeur, feeling weak and vulnerable as the old,
familiar sensation of desire raced through her.

Several pairs of jeans were strewn across a chair in
the corner of the room. Swiftly she lifted each, rifled
hastily through the pockets, becoming desperate with

every second that passed, because any moment he
would be sure to awake, be sure to catch her...

'Looking for this?'

Christy stiffened, straightened up and then turned
slowly back towards the bed. Drew was lying with his
head propped up on one hand, watching her. In the
other, held out like a bait, was the key to the car. For
a moment she felt faint. Her mouth had dried at the
first sound of his voice, her pulse raced fit to burst.
'I...I...' she floundered pitifully, struggling to come
up with anything that was vaguely coherent.

'Yes?' He wasn't going to make this easy. She could
see the gleam of white teeth against tanned skin and
knew that instantly. 'Am I to get an explanation,
Christy? Come on, try—it really will be rather enter-
taining watching you struggle to justify your actions.
Rifling through my belongings like a common thief?'
He gave a taunting shake of his head. 'Surely Christy
King wouldn't stoop quite so low as that.'

'She would if she were being held captive by an
egotistical swine who was hell-bent on some sort of
perverse therapy!' she snapped wildly.

'So,' Drew murmured carelessly, 'you want the
key—come over and take it from me.'

She had been about to leave, to fly out of the room
without a word. Now she turned, stood hesitantly in
the moonlight. 'W-what?'

Drew held up the key once again. 'You heard,
Christy—come and get it.'

He knew she would never dare. He just knew it.
Perhaps that was why she even considered risking it.
To go across and snatch the key from his hand without
a word, walk out of the room, escape. Oh, yes, now
that would be something!

She did it before she could think any more, before the possible consequences of her actions really occurred to her. He had expected her to decline his offer and that one fact spurred her on. Quick as a flash she crossed the room, stood beside the bed, careful to avert her eyes from the gleaming sensual body, and held out her hand. 'The key, then—if you please!'

Drew's mouth curled. 'Well, well, you have more spark than I credited you with!'

'So?' Christy held her hand out. It was shaking most dreadfully. Her eyes fixed on her pale, slender fingers and she did her best to steady them. 'Are you going to give me the keys or not?'

Drew gently placed the metal object into her palm, his hand still covering it, still holding it, so that infuriatingly Christy couldn't actually take the key. 'Maybe I've changed my mind,' he whispered teasingly; 'maybe I just wanted to see if you had the nerve.'

Christy glared. 'But . . . but you said——'

He slanted her an infuriating glance. 'Perhaps I lied.'

She snatched at his hand in a blaze of fury. 'Damn you, Drew Michaels! Damn you! Give me that key! You can't do this to me. You can't!' She caught at his hand and tried to prise open the fingers that were clasped tightly together. It was a futile gesture, but she kept on trying until quite suddenly the key dropped from his hand on to the crisp white sheet.

'OK, Christy, it's yours. It seems cruel to keep it from you when you want it so much. Take it. Go. Let me get some sleep.'

For a moment she just stood, clutching the key, watching as he adjusted his pillow and closed his eyes.

Was this it, then? she asked herself. Was he really going to allow her to leave?

She spun from the room, slamming the door for good measure on her way out. Her holdall was in her room, already packed. She picked it up and then ran like the wind, her feet clattering noisily on the worn wooden treads of the stairs.

Her nose wrinkled instinctively as she sat in the smelly battered car, but she didn't care. This vehicle was her escape route back to the real world, back to London and her friends, back to civilisation.

A world without Drew Michaels.

CHAPTER EIGHT

CHRISTY inserted the key and turned it. Nothing. She tried again. Not so much as a squeak. Again. Again. Each try was accompanied by a muttered fiery expletive.

He knew of course, she thought furiously, picturing his taunting smile; he had no intention of allowing her to leave. This was just one more episode in his mission to belittle her, to make her feel a fool. What had he done? Removed all the petrol? Taken some vital lead or wire?

Christy closed her eyes in despair and swore loudly and violently.

'Tut, tut! Such language, Christy! And there was I believing you to be a well-brought-up young woman!'

'Don't talk to me!' Christy flung open her eyes and tried to wrench open the door. It was stuck and she cursed again, aware that her blood-pressure was soaring and a coronary was probably on the cards. She glared at him, an almost luminous apparition in the moonlight with a gleaming white sheet wrapped casually around his waist. 'Just don't say one more word to me!' she yelled, as she finally managed to extricate herself from the smelly car. 'Not one word!'

'You didn't really imagine I'd let you go so easily?' Drew's voice was scathing. 'We've hardly been here more than a few hours after all.'

'Long enough for me!' Christy snapped. 'More than long enough.'

'Well, too bad!' White teeth gleamed amusingly in the dusky blackness. 'I plan to keep you my prisoner for a little while longer yet!'

'This is all just a silly infantile game to you, isn't it?' she demanded angrily. 'And for some weird reason you expect me to go along with it.'

'I expect nothing from you, Christy, absolutely nothing,' Drew informed her tersely. 'That way I can guarantee that I won't be disappointed! Now be a good little girl and run along back to bed, or you'll be all scratchy and irritable from lack of sleep in the morning!'

'Do you know something?' Christy muttered furiously, 'You are for sure the most patronising, arrogant, egotistical male——'

Drew snatched a hand out and caught her none too gently by the arm as she stormed past. 'Don't waste your breath, Christy,' he drawled. 'I've heard it all before—remember?'

'Time to get up!'

Christy rolled over in bed and peered bleary-eyed in the direction of his voice. Drew was standing framed in the doorway to her bedroom looking the picture of masculine health and vigour. 'Go away! I am not speaking another word to you—not after the dirty trick you played on me last night.' Christy pressed her face into the pillow and pulled the bedclothes over her head only to find them wrenched none too gently back off her in the next moment.

'Up!'

'No!' Christy muttered defiantly.

'Do as I say!' Drew's expression was set and firm. Quite, quite determined, she thought, as her eyes slid cautiously to his face. It was clear that he wasn't going to take no for an answer.

'What for?' she asked, still defiant, although playing for time now, because inevitably she would end up doing as Drew instructed—when he looked like this, she didn't dare defy him for long. 'Are we going somewhere? Back to London, for instance?'

'No.' Drew threw a pair of jeans and a shirt in her direction. 'We are going to do some work. Put these things on. Later, maybe, just maybe, if certain guests have pulled their weight sufficiently, we may go out on the loch for a couple of hours, take a picnic perhaps.'

'And I'm supposed to be enticed out of bed with that?' Christy enquired scornfully. 'What work?' she added, as an afterthought, suspicious suddenly.

'Get out of bed and you'll find out, won't you?' Drew replied, flinging the covers on to the floor, making her scramble to cover herself beneath the flimsy silk and lace nightdress she wore. 'Come on, I've got a decent breakfast waiting for you downstairs and if you don't hurry up it's going to get cold.'

'I can't eat all this!' Christy pushed her plate aside, only to find it pushed back in front of her.

'Try. You're going to need something more substantial inside you than coffee. You're not going to last more than ten minutes.'

Christy stared hopelessly at the large steaming plate of bacon, eggs, sausages and mushrooms that Drew had placed in front of her. He wasn't giving her any options. Get up or else, and now orders to eat what was put in front of her, as if she were a recalcitrant schoolgirl or something.

It did smell rather nice, she thought, reluctantly picking up her knife and fork. But what about all the calories, all the saturated fat?

'Are all your houses as spartan as this one?' Christy asked a minute or so later, in between mouthfuls of breakfast. She was enjoying the meal, she realised; it had been years since she had allowed herself to indulge this way. Most people assumed her svelte, lissom figure simply happened by chance, but she, like most women, had to work at the size-ten figure by watching what she ate and working out several times a week. Her eyes roamed around the interior of the kitchen as she spoke, resting on significant clues: the old deep stone sink in the corner, the wooden draining board that adjoined it, the complete lack of any surplus item that would indicate luxury in the twentieth century.

Drew stretched back in his chair, following her gaze. 'No, not at all. This is a kind of departure from my usual choice of abode.'

'All the others are as luxurious as the world has been led to believe, then?' Christy asked casually.

Drew's mouth curled. 'You make it sound as if I've got a place in every continent,' he drawled.

Christy raised enquiring brows. 'Haven't you?'

'No, of course not. That's just hype, generated by the media. I have three—no, four homes including this one. A couple of them are particularly impressive, I suppose. But this farmhouse, in its own way, is as beautiful as any of them. Elaborate decoration isn't for me. I decided to keep everything very simple here. It suits the surroundings, suits the general atmosphere of the place. My other homes are a mixture of styles. A reflection of my life at the time of purchase, I suppose.' He took a mouthful of coffee. 'My New York apartment, for instance—that has the most eclectic style of all my homes. I was rather mixed up when I bought that place.' He paused, reading Christy's expression accurately. 'Sounds grand maybe, but a couple of them are just apartments and they're really for convenience.' He gave a small shrug. 'I rather dislike having to stay in hotels when I travel. They have such an impersonal atmosphere.'

Christy shifted her gaze and forced down a forkful of mushrooms, wondering if the remark had been thrown at her deliberately. Why did you stay in one three years ago, then? she wanted to ask. Why?

'This work I'm supposed to be doing today,' she murmured after a moment's silence. 'What is it? Am I allowed to know now?'

Drew leant back in his chair. 'Don't look so apprehensive, you'll enjoy it. There's a small wood attached to this property. It needs clearing. I've started, but there's still a fair bit left to do.'

'Oh, you are kidding! You surely are not expecting me . . . ?' He was, of course, she saw that instantly. 'Surely you could get a contractor in to do it?' she said hastily, failing to imagine herself humping around logs, or thrashing away at undergrowth. 'They'd be sure to do a much better job, wouldn't they?'

Drew's lips curved. 'Maybe so, but where's the fun in that? Besides, a little hard physical work is very good for the soul, extremely therapeutic. You're going to benefit a great deal, Christy. In fact I'm sure you'll be absolutely indebted to me by the end of the day for giving you this opportunity.'

He thought it was funny and yet he was serious too at the same time. Christy threw him an extremely suspicious look.

A little while later after the breakfast things had been washed up—without the aid of a dishwasher—and the kitchen tidied she joined him outside and her worst suspicions were confirmed. He really did want to make a complete and utter fool of her.

'You don't honestly expect me to use an axe?'

Drew raised one dark eyebrow and lifted an extremely heavy-looking log on to a pile by the back door. 'Why not? I've sawed the wood into sizeable chunks. He placed a chump of wood on to a round flat stump of wood, used as a chopping-block, and swung the sizeable implement above his head. 'It's all in the swing. It will take you a few tries, but once you get the hang of it you'll be well away.'

Christy watched as gleaming muscle swung the axe expertly at the wood and split it into two pieces. 'Here, now you.'

It was as heavy and unwieldy as it looked. On her first attempt the swing was a joke and she missed not only the piece of wood that Drew had placed down for her but the chopping-block as well. She tried again. A fraction better this time. Then another go, forced on by Drew every time, until at last she managed to achieve her aim. 'There you are, you see,' Drew smiled. 'See what you can do, Christy, when you put your mind to it!'

She felt ridiculously pleased with herself, despite his patronising tone, quite inexplicably keen to have another go. A few attempts at the same piece of wood and then success and without a thought or a glance at Drew Christy the glamorous city girl was attacking

the next piece, totally absorbed suddenly by her unusual task.

By mid-morning she was an expert—well, almost
one, she thought, pleased that she could take her aim
and swing her axe with the best of them.

When Drew came over and handed her an ice-cold
glass of beer, she downed it as if she were a navvy.
'You're taking to this better than I thought,' he con-
fessed. 'Quite a bundle of contradictions, aren't you?'

'I am what I am!' Christy retorted spiritedly, annoyed by the familiar mocking tone in Drew's voice.

'And that is?'

She hesitated, partly because the inflection in his
voice had changed noticeably, making her feel self-
conscious, because suddenly it sounded as if he really
did want to know and partly because, if she were
honest, she really didn't have a clue where she was
coming from, going to... what sort of a person she
really was, really wanted to be...

Things had happened in her life; fate had seemed
to steer its own course. When she had left the children's home at sixteen she had been lucky enough to
fall straight into the hands of one of the finest and
most reputable model agencies in London—spotted
by a scout, given a contract, helped with the fright-
ening task of finding secure and sensible
accommodation.

Oh, yes! She thanked God a thousand times a day
even now for that most lucky of lucky breaks. If she
hadn't had the fortune of her good looks to help
her she really couldn't imagine what might
have happened ...

'I'm a career woman,' Christy replied finally, her expression wholly serious, 'who's getting by. Doing the best she can——'

'That statement doesn't sound as if it's coming from a very successful person,' Drew murmured with a dry smile. 'You've made it, Christy; why that element of undervaluation in your voice? You are, after all, the highest paid woman on British television.'

'If you think that all I'm concerned about is money——!' she retorted sharply.

He held up both hands in supplication. 'Now don't get so uptight, Christy. I didn't say a word. Just pointing out the fact that it's quite an achievement, something to be proud of—reaching the top of your profession, whatever the particular field may be.' He paused. 'It's not enough, though, is it?'

'What?' Christy threw him a sharp, slightly uneasy glance, because he had been reading her mind again, speaking her thoughts out loud.

'Money. Professional achievement,' he added. 'They're important enough, but they don't make the whole. Don't complete the puzzle.'

She arched her eyebrows in query, playing dense. She knew exactly what he meant, but she chose to play for time, because she wasn't sure she wanted to have a deep conversation with Drew Michaels about something as important as the meaning of life—she wasn't at all sure she could handle it. A puzzle. A jigsaw with parts still missing, not slotted into allotted place. Christy considered. She hadn't thought of it in quite that way before.

'Fame and fortune can be very shallow things, very artificial, can't they?' Drew continued.

'Can they?' Christy carefully placed her glass down on a garden bench, carefully avoided Drew's gaze. 'Am I to take it you're speaking from experience?'

'Oh, for sure.' The lightness of his tone belied the sudden intensity in his eyes. Christy, looking up, saw Drew's expression and found herself irresistibly intrigued.

She waited and when he said no more found herself asking with deliberate casualness, 'You want to elaborate?'

Drew's mouth curved. 'Do I detect Christy King the interviewer making an appearance?' he asked. 'Will what I say now be used in evidence against me?'

She looked at him, genuinely surprised. 'I'm just interested,' she answered honestly. 'Besides, I haven't got my tape recorder on me, so you can always categorically deny everything at a later date! I wouldn't have a leg to stand on.'

'What about turning the tables?' Drew enquired, a gleam of amusement in his eyes. 'This weekend has surprised us both in more ways than one. Why don't we continue the trend? Why don't you tell me a little about yourself? You were brought up in a children's home, I believe?'

Christy felt herself redden. 'How did you know that?'

He shrugged. 'Oh, I make it my business to find out certain things—if you're interested enough it isn't that difficult. What was life like?' he added, stemming the questions that Christy suddenly wanted to ask. Interested? How did he find out? Why? 'Did you know your parents at all?'

She felt dreadfully flustered, hot and ill at ease. He shouldn't be delving into her private life like this!

She took a swift breath. 'The answer is horrible and no! Look, this is ridiculous——' Christy opened her mouth to protest but Drew was well into his stride.

'What age were you when you left? How did you cope afterwards?'

'Sixteen and . . . and I coped OK. Look, will you stop this, Drew?' Christy muttered shakily, holding her head in her hands. 'Stop bombarding me with questions, for heaven's sake! I can't think straight.'

'Isn't this the Christy King technique? I thought the point was you rattled questions off one after another, once you'd tied your guests up in knots, and then the information just came tumbling out!' he queried with deliberate mild innocence. 'Isn't that right?'

'No, it is not!' Christy snapped, 'As you very well know! True, I sometimes do fire questions off, but only to politicians, slippery businessmen——' she glared at Drew pointedly '—people I don't like. Anyway I'm not here to be interviewed, you are!'

She turned to go back into the house; it was hot out here under the sun. Hot and sticky and tense. But Drew barred her way. 'We haven't finished working yet.'

'Tough!' Christy glared up into the broad, angular features and challenged him with her violet eyes. 'I'm worn out. I've had enough. Have you seen the disgusting state of my hands? Look at them!' She turned her palms uppermost and showed Drew the sore red calluses across the fleshy part just beneath her fingers.

Drew took her hands in his, rubbing gently over the swollen blisters. 'Nothing wrong with those! They just need toughening up a little. Good, honest working hands, Christy. A first for you, no doubt!' He was smiling but she felt the sting of his retort.

'Well, that's where you're wrong actually!' she replied swiftly, annoyed by his tone. 'It's taken me years to erase the awful grime and the weals that were a constant——'

She realised just in time. She had been about to reveal an aspect of life at the children's home, a depressing, painful aspect that had taken her years forcibly to forget. She spun away and would have fled, but for Drew's gently restraining hands.

'Let's have another beer, shall we?' he murmured casually, placing an arm lightly around Christy's shoulders. 'We can sit over there in the shade. You're right. It is too hot to work.'

She wasn't quite sure how Drew got the information out of her. At first there was silence while they lazed in the deep shade beneath some extremely gnarled old oak trees, drinking a little, enjoying the wonderful views out over the loch. Then gradually a little talk about safe things like whether there was the possibility it would rain and then some more silences, companionable this time until Drew broached the subject again.

'Why do you hate talking about your childhood, Christy?'

She didn't answer him immediately, afraid to use her voice, to talk about something that was so close and personal. 'I...I just find it difficult,' she murmured, after a long pause, deliberately not looking in his direction.

'Why?'

She hesitated. 'I just don't want to...to keep looking back into the past. It's gone. It's over.'

'Because you were so unhappy at the children's home. Because whoever was in charge treated the children in their care badly.'

It wasn't so much a question as a statement of fact. No one had actually come out and said as much to her before, mainly because she had always worked extremely hard at glossing over that time of her life. Now Drew had instinctively guessed, put two and two together. She felt a curious kind of release. She didn't want sympathy or anything, she didn't want to talk about it. She just felt glad suddenly that someone knew.

'Yes,' she answered with honest simplicity. 'That's right.'

'And you don't wish to talk about it?'

'No.' Christy risked a glance at him, her brow furrowed with concern. 'No. Please——'

Drew reached forward and laid a large reassuring hand on her arm. 'It's OK. You have my word that what little I know won't be passed on. Now!' He jumped up and pulled Christy to her feet. 'We've lazed around long enough. When I said it was too hot to work, I only meant out of doors. Barrett, my nearest neighbour, left a sack full of broad beans for me this morning. They need to be podded and frozen by nightfall. Come on, this will really finish your hands off once and for all!'

Christy tried to work out why she wasn't telling Drew what he could do with his broad beans. She had been shelling for what seemed like hours—*was* hours, she realised when she glanced at her wristwatch. Was it perhaps because the work was evenly divided? Drew

really was doing as much as if not more than she. Or
was it because as they worked Drew chatted, told her
a little of his life, a few amusing anecdotes about *his*
world? No great revealing secrets, of course, Christy
reflected, no personal thoughts, just stuff about his
early childhood, his parents' way of life, his school.
It was absorbing, though, despite the fact that it had
been reasonably well-documented before, mostly because it was in such marked contrast to her own
upbringing.

'Right; finished. And if I ever have to shell a broad
bean again it will be too soon.' Drew leant back in
his chair and stretched his arms high above his head.

'Why do you do it?'

'What exactly?' Drew threw Christy an enquiring
glance.

'This! All that!' Christy pointed to the pile of empty
bean husks, gestured outside to where the wood was
neatly stacked by the kitchen door. 'You don't have
to. You could afford to employ an army of helpers,
or buy everything in.' She shook her head and
shrugged. 'I just don't understand.'

Drew gave her a considered look. 'You know, the
having of money is a peculiar thing,' he murmured.
'When I was a young, struggling actor, fresh out of
drama academy, it was almost all I could think
about—what I would buy, do once I had made a name
for myself, once I had made it to the top. My family,
you see, decided that I should forge my way in the
world without their help. My decision to become an
actor hadn't really gone down too well with them and
so I had to struggle the same as anyone else, despite
all my so-called advantages.'

'They didn't help you at all?'

'Not at all. You think that's wrong?' Drew asked. He shook his head. 'I don't. At the time, of course, I didn't understand, but now I see that if I had had everything handed to me on a plate my whole career just wouldn't have got off the ground. I had to fight for everything—out of necessity, because I had to eat, live. The urgency wouldn't have been there if I had trotted off at intervals when things got a bit tough to ask my parents for a little something to tide me over.' He paused and Christy could see him thinking, remembering, going over the old days in his mind. 'Well, anyway, in the end I did manage to get some lucky breaks, make a name for myself...' He looked across at Christy and smiled, a brilliant heart-stopping affair that had her melting in her seat. 'Hell! I'm rambling. Let's just say that I'm touching thirty now. I'm a millionaire more times over than I really want to know and I often yearn back to those days when I hardly knew how I was going to feed myself.'

'You're surely not trying to re-create poverty?' Christy asked, clearly horrified at the idea.

'No, I don't think so,' Drew murmured drily. 'If that were the case I would have to say I was managing to do a very bad job of it. Four homes, a plane, a yacht?' He smiled indulgently and she felt the teeniest bit foolish. 'No, that's not it. I enjoy my wealth. I'm grateful for it. But I need this place, these tasks to bring me down to earth, to remind me what real life is all about. It's all too easy to get swept away on a tide of absolute unreality in my business...in *our* business,' he added pointedly.

She saw the look in his eyes and knew what he was thinking. 'You're suggesting that that's what I've done?' Her voice was defensive, frosty.

Drew's eyes met hers in a probing stare. 'I think that yes, on occasions you have...' he paused, searching for the right set of words '...lost touch with who you are, where you're coming from.'

'Why don't you just come right out and say that I'm a big-headed, superior snob? A shallow, pretentious show-off? Something along those lines? That's what you're so politely suggesting, isn't it?'

'You're angry now because I've spoken the truth.' He sounded disappointed and that, somehow, made everything worse. 'It's an easy thing to do, Christy, to lose yourself—don't get me wrong, I'm not trying to get one over on you. Believe me, I've been there, fallen into that obsessive trap myself. You live your life at a frenetic, crazy pace, get caught up in a world, a lifestyle which only judges people on superficial things like status, wealth, looks——'

'You're right.' Christy's voice was quietly calm. What was the point in being angry? She wasn't a fool. Sometimes, on a very few occasions, she had managed to stand back, view herself from a distance, see that there were some parts of her that bore no relation to how she felt deep inside. She hadn't lost her way exactly, she had just strayed on to the wrong path, got side-tracked here and there by the glamour, the utter unbelievable contrast with her early, unpromising years...

Drew's mouth curved into the most unbelievable smile. 'I am?'

Christy, for some totally ridiculous reason, found herself grinning too. 'Yes, although it sticks in my throat to say it.' She lifted her hand in acknowledgement. 'On occasion I have found myself being...well, let's just say being someone else. You know of course

that you bring out the worst in me. Yesterday while
we were walking...' Her voice trailed away.
'Well...I'm not...I'm really not quite like that, quite
so...'

'Cantankerous?'

Christy pursed her lips in mock-annoyance. 'No.
Look, I haven't the first idea how we got on to this
subject but I think it's time we thought about food.'
She rose with determination from the table, began
clearing the debris of empty broad-bean pods. 'You
have got something for us to eat beside broad beans,
I take it?' she asked with a briskness that didn't fool
either of them.

She had been affected by their conversation more
than she could say. Somehow Drew had managed to
penetrate the barriers, managed to make her admit to
things that were so dreadfully personal... She shook
her head disbelievingly as she cleared the table.

Drew saw her expression and smiled.

'Take the oars. Now get them level and angle them
into the water. That's it; good.'

They were on the loch. It was evening and Christy's
body felt as if it had gone ten rounds in the boxing
ring. She ached all over. She felt more tired than she
had ever thought possible—until yesterday, that was.
And now here she was rowing herself and Drew out
into the middle of the loch.

She glanced around her, at the way the low sun
glinted on the surface of the water, making it appear
like liquid gold, and immediately lost her rhythm with
the oars. She was secretly rather proud of herself. She
had never attempted anything like this before and yet
she was doing remarkably well.

'It's been a day for firsts, hasn't it?' Drew remarked, leaning back casually into the bow of the
boat. 'You realise we've worked alongside one another
without any hint of anger or violence!'

'Don't speak too soon,' Christy murmured,
breathing hard; 'there's still time! I may still feel
compelled to throw myself over the side of this boat!
Look,' she added, with just a hint of pleading in her
voice that would never have been allowed to surface
twenty-four hours ago, 'can you do this now? I'm
absolutely worn out! My shoulders have begun to seize
up already.'

It was the first time she had asked him for anything, had spoken to him with a natural lightness in
her voice. She handed Drew the oars and wondered
if he had noticed the change too. A minute incident
perhaps, but a somehow significant one all the same.

Christy found herself watching him as he rowed
them both out into the middle of the loch. A weird
sort of peace had fallen over her and she couldn't, try
as she might, find an explanation for it. All her pent-
up anger had disappeared. All the facts remained the
same, she hadn't lost her memory or anything, but
still she couldn't conjure up the spiky animosity that
had fuelled their relationship from the word go. It's
because I'm tired, she thought swiftly, turning to look
how far they had come, leaning over and trailing her
hand in the cool water. That's what it must be.

'There's an inlet just over here. We'll go ashore and
eat. You are hungry, I take it?'

Christy glanced up. She had been drifting, allowing
her mind free rein, thinking about their conversation
this afternoon and, inevitably, about that time three
years ago in Drew's hotel room. She still hadn't

worked out how to handle it, handle the memories. She still hadn't worked out why it bugged her so, all these years later... 'I'm sorry?'

A smile tugged the corners of Drew's mouth. 'It wasn't important, Christy. Carry on dreaming. You look quite delectable, lying back like that. A feast for the eyes. That dress suits you rather well.'

She had changed for this excursion. Back to the powder-blue outfit, which heightened the colouring of her eyes, flattered the lightly tanned skin of her throat and arms. 'Anything was better than the outfit you gave me to wear this morning,' she replied jauntily, realising with annoyance that she had blushed at his compliment. 'I felt like a stranger in those clothes.'

'You looked like one,' Drew threw back at her. 'Quite a shock to see Christy King in something other than designer labels! No, I'm not getting at you again,' he added swiftly, 'so you can take that defensive expression off your face. Which, by the way, still looks a hundred times better without all that gunge you usually slap on.'

'It's hardly gunge!' Christy retorted, picturing the beautifully packaged make-up Drew had tossed in the river yesterday. 'And I don't slap it on!' She allowed a small smile. 'Make-up is artfully applied,' she informed him with mock-seriousness. 'You put on enough to bring out your best features, but not so much that you look like a clown.' She wondered if the latter was how he would have described her. Did she really wear too much? Sure, she liked her glossy red lipstick, but that was mainly for studio work, for the glamorous image she projected on screen. She made sure everything was extremely muted for everyday. Clearly, though, she thought, her idea of muted and Drew's were poles apart. 'I do feel dreadfully naked,' she admitted, bringing up a hand to touch her cheek.

Drew's eyes sparkled. 'If only!' he teased.

They ate right near the edges of the loch, sitting on a grassy bank that was sheltered by a cluster of young trees, which, Drew informed her, he had planted himself some weeks previously.

Christy hugged her arms close around her knees and watched with Drew in silence as the sun, a huge ball of burning orange, sank slowly, inch by inch, beneath the glistening water.

It was a memorable moment. Christy knew it, felt it. Total peace all around. No cars, no noisy radios, no people. Just the two of them, alone.

A surge of exhilaration rushed through her as the last glowing rays of the sun slipped away. Something was happening. Something inside, something monumental and irrepressible. She felt as if she had found that thing, that piece of the puzzle, the missing part of herself, her life.

She felt almost frightened by the intensity of feeling, by the fact that she didn't understand, couldn't sensibly reason with herself. What was going on? The day had been so strange, so different. She had started off believing it would be one of the worst days of her life and yet now, so many hours later, she felt as if she had been a prisoner all these years and only now, now had her shackles been removed. Only now had she that feeling of freedom deep within.

When she turned to face Drew he looked at her for a moment without speaking and then slowly, care-

fully, as if she were a very precious piece of china, he
pulled her towards him.

He held her for a long while, drawing her close, so
that she sat cradled on his lap, enfolded totally in the
circle of his arms, and then he tilted her chin with
one gentle finger and lowered his lips to meet hers.

'You're crying,' he whispered huskily, pressing his
mouth against the salty wetness on her cheeks. 'You
shouldn't do that. Not now, not when everything's so
perfect.' He laid Christy back down on the rug, ar-
ranging the strands of her hair which were splayed all
around her face in a halo of gold. 'Now,' he whispered, gazing deep into her eyes, 'now is the right
time.'

He bent his head and kissed her lips with a long,
slow, completely erotic command. On and on, until
Christy felt her senses reeling, until she felt the ache
and the need for him so acutely that she thought she
would die with wanting. On and on, so that she
wanted desperately for him to touch her, for him to
take all the pleasure she was offering.

Eagerly she took hold of his hand, pressed it fer-
vently to her breast, willing him with all her movements to caress and touch the most intimate parts of
her.

'Don't hurry things, Christy. We have all night.
Slowly, slowly. Like this. See?'

She did see. Drew supported her back and tilted her
into a sitting position so that she could watch as his
fingers slid beneath the thin straps of her dress, pulling
them inch by inch from her shoulders. Slowly, oh, so
slowly further downwards. Lower and lower until the
paler skin of her breasts began to be revealed. Lower
again, each little movement producing a sharp aching

need, a sensation that was so indescribably wonderful that Christy shuddered with the power of it.

Drew teased the edges of her dress away, so that she was erotically revealed to him. Christy looked down, then gazed into his face, saw the concentrated intensity of his expression, the need for her, and felt exultant, gloriously brazen, powerful because her body could generate such mutual pleasure.

But of course this was just the beginning. She shuddered as Drew tugged the fabric roughly downwards, finally revealing her full breasts in all their glory; shivered with delight as his hands removed the rest of her clothing and then his own, as they caressed and moulded and then began a journey of the most sensational kind, teasing her, tormenting her just like before with delicate touches that made her gasp aloud.

Three years ago she had known him to be a master of the art of lovemaking; now she knew that this was even better than before, even more mind-blowing. Special. Perfect.

He penetrated her with an ease and gentleness that was as skilful as she would have expected. He moved with an expertise born, she knew, of practice but found she didn't care. He might have made love to many other women, but he couldn't have done it with such tenderness, with such feeling. She sensed that knowledge totally as he brought her to that peak of delicious ecstasy and held her there, on the edge, so that the full wonder of the moment could be kept and savoured for as long as possible.

When the glorious release arrived for them both he gripped her fiercely, showered her face with kisses and then he opened his eyes and smiled. 'Worth waiting for, I hope?'

Christy nodded, totally unable to speak, her violet eyes glistening with emotion.

They lay for a long time without a word and looked up at the darkening sky. Pin-points of light heralded the evening that had crept up on them unawares. Christy snuggled against the strength of Drew's chest and sighed.

'Feel good?'

'Mmm.' She snuggled up a little closer and closed her eyes. 'I feel glorious. Could we stay here, just like this, all night?'

'I don't believe I'm hearing this!' Drew bent and kissed the tip of her nose. 'You actually want to sleep out in the open, with all this nature?'

'I do.' Christy smiled and pressed her face against the cotton of Drew's shirt, nibbled the skin beneath teasingly. 'We could swim. It's a glorious evening and the loch's so still, so peaceful-looking.'

'It will be cold,' Drew warned, as Christy sat up, 'and we haven't anything to dry ourselves on.' He pulled her back down beside him. 'No, we'll go back to the house. But not yet.' His hand found her breast, she felt the hardened length of him, pressing firmly, tellingly against her suppliant body.

She knew he wanted her again.

Later, much later, Drew rowed them back across the loch. It was very dark now. Inky. Christy realised she had never known such thick blackness. In the town and cities there was always that unnatural glow of street-lamps, of other people's houses. You couldn't escape the light, couldn't escape the unending activity. And she had never wanted to—up to now. The thought that she would have to return to her insane, frenetic existence made her feel curiously sad. Surely not? she asked herself, examining the emotion. You love your world; your house, your work, your friends ...

She found herself gazing at Drew's solid outline and the thoughts which filled her mind then were so unexpected she thrust them away from her in panic. She would not think any more tonight. She would just enjoy, allow herself to feel secure in the knowledge that what had happened between Drew and herself this evening had been something that they had both wanted. In the morning, with the new day adding its harsh light of reality, she would examine her feelings more closely, try and secure some sort of indication from Drew about how he felt, whether there was maybe some sort of future for the two of them ...

They had both alighted and Drew was tying the rowing boat securely to the small jetty, when the unmistakable sound of a vehicle's tyres could be heard, scrunching along the gravel track towards the farmhouse. The headlights came into view in the next moment and soon a battered Land Rover had pulled to a halt in front of them.

Christy saw Drew flash his torchlight in its direction and then he hurriedly approached the vehicle.

She wondered all the usual things—who? Why? Where from?—but waited patiently, convinced that after a short interval she would be acquainted with all the necessary facts. After all, it was rather late. Past eleven, she estimated, and this surely was no ordinary visit.

Drew hadn't bothered to lock the farmhouse—that was another wonderful thing about living out here, she acknowledged swiftly; nine times out of ten there was absolutely no need to worry about locking every single thing up, about barring the way to people you saw maybe every single day, but still couldn't trust. Christy thought of her multitude of locks at home in London, the complicated phone mechanism on her front door, and sighed as she entered the kitchen; the world was slowly going crazy, turning bad, and there didn't seem to be much anyone could do about it.

'Christy, something important's come up. I've got to go.' Drew burst into the room a few moments later and delved into a pot that stood on the windowsill, bringing out a bunch of keys. 'Go to bed now and hopefully...' he paused and looked grim suddenly '...hopefully I'll be back with you some time tomorrow.' He was heading back out of the door as he spoke.

'Drew!' Christy ran out into the darkness after him, half colliding with the bulky figure of a man, who she presumed was Barrett. 'Drew! What's the matter? What's going on?'

He had disappeared around the other side of the house. Around to where several outbuildings stood. From the light, shed through the uncurtained kitchen window, she could see Drew opening the double doors, making his way around what looked like a car. A car! Christy heard the engine roar into life, a throaty noise that indicated something fast and powerful. All along he had had that thing here?

'I'll explain when I get back.' He had brought the low, sleek vehicle to a halt beside her. 'Be patient.' He snaked a hand out through the car window and pulled her swiftly down towards him, kissing Christy with rough haste full on the mouth. 'See you!'

And with that and a roar of the car's engine he was gone.

CHAPTER NINE

CHRISTY stared after the glowing tail-lights for several unbelieving minutes.

Barrett, the neighbouring farmer, tapped her lightly on the shoulder. 'I didn't mean to frighten you, miss,' he murmured. 'I'll be off now. Mr Michaels said he'll phone and tell me if there's any news he wants passing on.'

Christy recovered herself as best she could, gathering what wits she had still intact and said swiftly, tugging at the man's sleeve as he turned to go, 'Please. C-could you tell me what this is all about? Is there some emergency? Is that what's happened?'

'Aye... well...' The man hesitated, clearly in some dilemma, and Christy realised she had put him into an awkward position. 'I'm sure Mr Michaels will tell you all he thinks you should know when he gets back. I'm sworn to secrecy, see, and I would'na want to break his confidence. We get along fine. He trusts me. Being as famous as he is, ye know, means he has to be careful. Journalists, see,' he confided quietly, 'dreadful bunch. They'd follow him morning noon and night if he let 'em! Still, as I say,' the old man continued with an awkward smile, 'when he gets back he'll no doubt tell you all about it. I should'na fret, my dear.' He turned then and began walking back to the Land Rover.

Christy hurried after him anxiously. The thought had rushed into her mind and she knew it was the one solution to this crazy, unbelievable mess she had got herself into. 'Could you possibly do me a favour?' she asked; her voice sounded hesitant, slightly breathless, like a little lost schoolgirl instead of the immensely successful career woman she was. 'You see, my...my old car's here. Drew started working on it, but I wouldn't want, now he's gone, to be left here alone without any transport and I wondered if you could possibly take a quick look at it for me. I'm sure it's something simple,' she added hastily; 'just a loose wire, or a lead...'

The farmer was only too pleased to oblige. He lifted the bonnet of the old Cortina and spotted the trouble immediately. Not that it would have taken an expert to work out the reason why the car wouldn't start, Christy thought drily; Drew, devious man that he was, had removed the battery.

She vented a sigh of frustration, cursing her own stupidity for not having the sense to inspect the engine herself. If she had done that in the beginning, things might well have turned out quite differently.

It took less than five minutes for Barrett to inspect the outhouses and return with the car's battery. Two more and it was back in place. Christy turned the keys, which were still in the ignition, and the car fired up into life immediately.

'Thank you so much,' she said, relief apparent in every syllable. 'You've saved my sanity.'

It was true. She watched as the Land Rover rumbled away and wondered what she would have done if the car hadn't been fixed. Walk? Hitch? Throw herself into the loch? Now at least she could count on making a swift and infinitely defiant exit. When Drew returned he would find the house empty and her long gone.

She turned and walked back into the kitchen. Fifteen minutes before and she had been in seventh heaven. And now? Well, now she was able to acknowledge the euphoric effects of Drew's expert lovemaking. She had been caught hook, line and sinker. Landed. Her mind shied away from the phrase but she forced herself to say it—laid—again. Christy closed her eyes and felt the sting of tears burning beneath the lids. What a fool she had been. Swayed, tricked by atmosphere and timing and Drew's instinctive expertise. She shook her head. He had left her with the words, 'Be patient.' He had said, 'See you!' Why hadn't he taken her with him? Why hadn't he explained what was happening? Why hadn't he held her close and murmured the words she most wanted to hear?

Because you mean absolutely nothing to him, that's why! Christy told herself with masochistic bluntness. He's used you. Face the facts. Stand up and look the truth straight in the eyes for once in your pathetic life! You were a challenge. He wanted revenge. He took both and now he's driven off into the night without a word of explanation.

Christy opened her eyes and wondered for the first time whether there indeed was any emergency. Could he have arranged the whole thing? Asked his friend and neighbour to come over, call him away?

She pictured Drew with his wad of notes the previous day, buying his way out of trouble with the old Cortina. This man Barrett maybe wasn't a friend; maybe he had been paid to do it. One hundred, two hundred pounds, it was nothing to Drew, absolute chicken feed, but to a farmer trying to scratch a living from the land it was a very pleasant amount of money, especially when all you had to do to earn it was drive four miles or so down the road and lie a little.

Christy's heart felt like lead as she got into the stinking Cortina and drove away from the farm-house. She glanced in her rear-view mirror as the craggy stone building became more and more difficult to see and felt the tears finally cascading down her cheeks.

'Hi! How was your stay?' Lizzie removed Christy's silk shawl and ushered her into the chaotic living-room. 'Did you do the impossible and manage to break through the Drew Michaels wall of stony silence?'

Christy removed a pile of books and slumped down on to the squashy bright red sofa. She had spent the whole of yesterday at home trying to work out what she would say when somebody asked her these sorts of questions and she still found she didn't have a clue.

'It . . .' She cleared her throat awkwardly. 'It didn't quite go according to plan, I'm afraid.'

Lizzie handed Christy a brimming glass of cool white wine and flopped down into a chair opposite. 'Oh?' she queried casually, taking a sip from her glass. 'What happened?'

Christy forced her expression to stay featureless, welcomed the dry freshness of the Chianti against her parched throat, and wondered fleetingly about the possibility of getting completely blotto, here in Lizzie's company. Perhaps it would take away the pain. Perhaps, just for a moment, she would be able to forget about the fact that she had made a complete fool of herself over a man who wasn't worth it.

No, she thought hastily, placing the glass carefully down on to a side-table, getting drunk never solved anything. It would only be sure to make matters worse, because there was, while she was under the influence, the risk that she would blab everything out, break down in a paroxysm of tears at Lizzie's feet, and one thing she had vowed she wouldn't do was tell anyone how it had really been. After all she had her pride.

'He flew us to Scotland in his plane,' Christy murmured.

'And you managed it?' Lizzie's eyes were wide with surprise.

'Just about.' She forced a smile and stared into Lizzie's animated face. If she thought this was exciting, what on earth would her reaction be to the rest of it? she wondered. 'I was pretty scared in the beginning. More so,' she added neutrally, 'when we hit a storm and Drew was forced to make an emergency landing.'

'No!' Lizzie's face was a picture of the most amazed astonishment. 'You mean you *crashed*?'

Christy shook her head a little and released a steadying breath. 'No, not anything as bad as that. But once we were down we had to walk miles, sleep out in the open...' She shook her head. 'It was horrific.'

'You're kidding!'

'Lizzie, believe me, I really wish I were! I never want to go through that again. The whole experience was absolutely horrendous.'

'But Drew's OK?' Lizzie asked swiftly. 'And you, you look fit enough. No injuries?'

Only my broken heart, Christy thought silently. Just that. 'No. We both came out pretty much unscathed. I hurt my knee a little——'

'Oh, what was he like? Do tell me!' Lizzie broke in urgently. 'Was he cool and magnificent in your moment of crisis just like he was in the films?'

Oh, dear God! I can't take any more of this! Christy pressed a trembling hand to her lowered head. I'm nowhere near strong enough. She took a deep breath and then looked up.

'He was fine, Lizzie. Just like any man, I suppose,' she replied casually. 'Bossy, arrogant, thought he knew best all the time.' She managed a light shrug. 'You can imagine the sort of thing, I'm sure. Macho behaviour at its most annoying.'

'And?'

Christy watched Lizzie's animated features and forced herself to continue. If she didn't, Lizzie, old friend that she was, would be sure to suspect that something was up. 'We finally found an old farmer. Drew borrowed his car and he drove us on to his place...' It came out well, all very matter-of-fact. Lizzie, she saw, didn't suspect a thing.

'So how long have you been back? I tried phoning yesterday but there was no reply.'

'I pulled the lead out,' Christy replied honestly. 'It was quite an exhausting two days. I needed a rest.'

'Traumatic too!' Lizzie shook her head in disbelief. 'Honestly! What an adventure! I'm astounded. Absolutely astounded. Have the newspapers got hold of it? They'll have a field day——'

'No! Lizzie, don't even think about it, please!'

'But the publicity, Christy!' Lizzie's public relations brain was working fast. Her eyes sparked with energy. 'It would be quite astronomical. Think of the effect. You've been talking about trying to break into America. Drew's a big star there. It could be just the opening you need!'

'Lizzie, I said no!' Christy repeated firmly, fighting hard to keep her composure. She felt sick at the very thought of Lizzie's suggestion, shocked too; she had never really noticed this hardened ruthless streak before. 'Besides, I'm not interested in all that any more. I just want to carry on working quietly here——'

'But Christy——!'

She rose, stemming the protests. 'I really think I should go, Lizzie. I only called around to fill you in and let you know I'm back.'

'Oh, yes, of course!' Lizzie scrambled up hastily and opened the front door. She glanced at Christy's simple evening attire: floaty coral trousers, topped by a plain white silk shirt. 'Are you meeting someone— Conrad?' she added.

'No, not tonight.' Christy smiled and then bent and kissed Lizzie's cheek. 'I'm going to go for a drive, out into the country somewhere. I'll maybe find a small, quiet restaurant where I can eat.'

'Christy? Everything is all right, isn't it?'

A perfectly normal, reassuring smile met Lizzie's slightly frowning expression. 'Of course!' she answered gaily—too gaily. 'What on earth could possibly be wrong?'

She drove like a demon until she reached the wide open spaces of the countryside. Then she parked her Jaguar and strolled for a while through a village full of pretty houses, where honeysuckle tumbled over gates and jasmine filled the warm night air with its sweet, heavy scent. Then she ate in a tiny restaurant where the patron seemed to greet the arrivals, cook and serve on table, and then with a heavy heart she returned to her car and forced herself to head back to London.

The phone began ringing just as she came through the front door. Christy stared at it, knew with the utmost certainty that it was him. He had called twice before, leaving a message on the answerphone that was short and sharp, simply stating in clipped tones that he had phoned, that he wished to speak to her.

A couple of seconds of indecision and then she picked up the receiver. 'Hello.' Her voice wasn't quiet. It didn't sound nervous or cautious. It came out sounding strong and confident, as if this were going to be just another run-of-the-mill telephone conversation, as if Drew were any old business contact with a penchant for calls in the early hours. How can I do it? she wondered, gripping the receiver tightly. How can I sound like this when inside I feel as if I'm going crazy?

'Christy?' His voice sounded worse than she had anticipated—cold and hard—and she felt a pang of regret because deep down a part of her had harboured the hope that he might just sound relieved, pleased, ecstatic at making contact with her at last. 'You left—why?'

The bluntness of his question took her aback for a couple of seconds. She listened to the silence and frantically tried to think of something to say. 'Because I...I don't like being abandoned,' she managed finally. 'I don't relish being left alone in the middle of nowhere, without an adequate explanation!'

'Don't you think that if I could have given you one I would have?' His voice sounded quietly grim.

'And what is that supposed to mean?' Christy enquired scathingly. 'Are you expecting me to believe that you didn't know why you were being called away?'

'No, that's not what I meant. But circumstances dictate——'

'Don't give me that! It was just another carefully calculated punishment in the sequence of events, wasn't it?' Christy continued tightly. 'The ultimate humiliation! When did you get the idea for that one? Before or after we made love? I must say your friend Barrett played his part exceedingly well, very convincing, I thought. You'll have to use him again, Drew, when you get yourself in another spot of bother!'

She should have made that her parting shot. Should have slammed the phone down on him then, but of course she didn't. Like a fool she hung on, breathing heavily, waiting hopefully, hating herself for being so pathetic, for giving him one last chance to make her think something . . . anything else.

There was a moment of deep silence. When Drew finally spoke, she knew it was the end.

'Well, well, Christy, you really do have it all worked out, don't you?' he murmured sarcastically. 'You really do believe I'd go to all that trouble—drive back and forth, cover hundreds of miles—just to prove some sort of sadistic point!' He gave a short, harsh laugh. 'You really have got an ego problem! And there was I imagining you'd do as I asked, trust me even! Well, I don't think I'll bother to keep you from your bed any longer, Christy. I apologise for phoning at such a late hour but I have an early flight tomorrow, or rather this morning. I'm off to Australia for a couple of months to do some filming. Oh, and by the way, in your hurry to escape you left your precious holdall at the farmhouse. I've sent it on. You should receive it within the next couple of days.'

The click in the earpiece told Christy the connection had been severed. Good! she thought fiercely. Good! Good! Good!

She placed the ornate receiver carefully back on to its cradle and then sank on to her knees and burst into tears.

'You really are the most gorgeous woman I have ever set eyes on.'

Christy gently placed her head against Conrad's shoulder and allowed herself to relax. 'Am I?' she murmured vaguely. 'Thank you, Conrad. It's very nice of you to say so.' He was a good dancer—just another one of his talents—but the feel of his arms around her slender waist did nothing for her.

How would Drew dance? she wondered. How would it feel now if his arms were holding her, touching her, pressing her close against his irresistible male length now? She would never know—never get a chance to find out. That was over, or rather it had never even begun. All her hopes, all just a pathetic dream...

Conrad moved smoothly and lightly but she wasn't aware of him at all. Drew. That was all she could think of. She couldn't get him out of her mind. Day and night. Awake or asleep. No respite from the memories of how wonderful it had been in that moment by the loch. How awful it was now.

She half shook her head in disgust at herself, at her own weakness. Drew was out of bounds. Out of her life. Out of the hemisphere even. He had been in Australia, or at least she presumed he was still there, for over four weeks now. Four whole weeks since that phone call. It felt like four years.

'Happy?' Conrad's voice was close. Christy thought she felt the fleeting brush of his mouth on her hair.

This was crazy. What was she doing to the poor man? Christy screwed her eyes shut and fought against her reaction to pull away from his arms. She should never have accepted this invitation. She should never have accepted all the other ones either. He was beginning to get the wrong idea, despite her repeated, fervent declarations that she didn't want a serious relationship, that he couldn't expect anything from her except friendship.

'I'm very thirsty, Conrad.' Christy jerked her head from his shoulder and managed to put some space between them. 'Do you think you could get me a drink?'

'Of course!' Conrad's expression showed concern as he scrutinised her face. 'You do look a little pale. Are you feeling all right?'

This was her chance. They could both leave now and go back to her place and then she would explain to Conrad tell him there was little point in him harbouring hopes of a lasting liaison.

She opened her mouth to speak, framing the sentence carefully in her mind so that he wouldn't get the wrong idea, when from somewhere over her left shoulder she heard *the* voice, *that* voice, the deep, personalised accent that sounded like no other, that contributed, in its small way, to making up the in-

credibly unique, magnetic figure that was Drew
Michaels.

'Oh, she's all right, Conrad, believe me! Christy
King's tougher than she looks. That fragile exterior
surrounds an inner core that has to be made of
tungsten carbide at the very least!'

His tone was as dry as a desert. Clipped and exceedingly cool. When Christy spun round she saw his
expression matched the voice—the jawline was
clenched, the generous mouth taut and lacking in any
humour, the eyes... She found herself gazing into
their blazing depths and felt herself grow hot and cold.
They glittered with a million messages, transferring
energy and yet sapping her of any strength all at the
same time. She felt sick with shock and yet she was
aware too of elation running alongside it, because he
was here, consuming her with his gaze, making time
stand still. He was here. If she reached out a hand
she could touch him...

'Aren't you going to ask me about Australia,
Christy?' he asked with a casual smile. 'What's the
matter? Don't tell me the cat has finally got your
tongue!'

He looked spectacular tonight, dressed with a casual
kind of elegance that most men could never quite pull
off. She had already, in that first moment of recog-
nition, catalogued his clothes: chinos, the fitted navy
jacket that accentuated the breadth of his shoulders,
the chambray shirt, undone as usual at the throat,
revealing as always the thick mass of hair at the very
base that somehow managed to set her senses on
fire...

Christy swallowed back the lump in her throat and
licked her lips nervously, a million thoughts bom-

barding her brain. How could he be here? she wondered frantically. How could he have found her? Why had he come?

She took a deep breath and managed to tear her eyes away from his face to glance nervously at Conrad. He looked a little confused, unsure about whether to be annoyed at this rude interruption or pleased because Drew, the big star, had deigned to honour them with his company.

They shook hands. Christy watched, saw the marked contrast between them—Drew so tall and dark with his muscular build, Conrad slight and fair—and she waited, trepidation consuming her.

'So, did Christy tell you about our little weekend away together?' Drew asked, once the two men had dispensed with the usual formalities.

'Conrad doesn't want to hear about that!' Christy's voice was sharp, pleading. She cast a bitter glance in Drew's direction. 'Nothing much happened anyway. He'd be bored beyond belief!'

Drew's mouth curved into a smile that made Christy feel suddenly very faint. He wouldn't, would he? she thought desperately, waiting and watching while he kept her teetering on the brink. He wouldn't actually tell Conrad all about that weekend? As far as Conrad was concerned the weekend had gone reasonably well. When he had enquired not long after she had returned, she had fobbed him off with a reply that was vague in the extreme and hurried him on to another subject.

'Conrad, would you very much mind getting me that drink?' she asked croakedly, smiling desperately across at him. 'I do feel dreadfully warm.'

'Yes, of course.' Conrad was all concern immediately and, with a slightly perplexed glance at Drew, immediately turned towards the house.

'He's very well-trained, isn't he?' Drew murmured, watching Conrad over the rim of his glass, as he weaved his way through the crowds on the patio. 'Does he always move as quickly as that when you say jump?'

'He cares about me!' Christy retorted heatedly. 'He's a very nice man.'

'Nice?' Drew slanted dark brows, his mouth curving into a mocking smile. 'Nice? Since when was that something to be proud of?'

'Oh, don't worry,' Christy retorted harshly; 'I realise that attributes such as the ones Conrad possesses aren't deemed attractive in your book. To be thoughtful and kind—oh, no!'

She spun away from him. She was breathing too hard, allowing Drew to see that his presence was upsetting her, but she couldn't help herself. She had thought about him, about all the things he had put her through, non-stop for the past four weeks, and now he was here . . .

'I always knew you were a sick, sadistic bastard!' She regained some of her composure and turned to face him again. 'What the hell do you think you're doing here?'

Drew slanted dark brows in puzzlement. He lifted his broad shoulders nonchalantly. 'I'm simply fulfilling a social engagement.'

Christy shook her head. 'Don't give me that! You weren't invited! This is on the B list as far as charity parties go; you know that as well as I do!'

'I'm not interested in categorising social invitations, Christy. If I want to attend I do, regardless of whether it's seen as being above or beneath my social status!' Drew informed her crisply. 'I know the host personally. We go back quite a long way in fact. I usually promise to show my face for a few minutes each year if I'm around, as it's for a worthy cause——'

'I would hardly have put you down as being interested in the battered wife type!' Christy retorted scathingly. 'You came along just to cause trouble, didn't you? Just to make my life a misery!' she hissed more quietly beneath her breath as a group of people passed by with interested glances. 'Why won't you leave me alone? Isn't it enough that you've done what you've done to me without this?'

The angled jaw hardened perceptively. She saw the anger flash across his face. 'I came because I was invited and because I wanted to support this particular area of fund-raising!' Drew informed her curtly. 'Don't start getting things out of proportion, Christy! We've already discussed the dangers of losing touch with reality, remember?' He gave her a disdainful look. 'It seems that it only takes a few weeks and you're back to your bad narcissistic old ways—as well, it seems, as adding paranoia to your list of faults!'

She couldn't answer him. Couldn't do anything other than stare stony-faced while she battled against revealing any expression other than anger and animosity.

'I believe our interview has finally been rescheduled?'

Christy nodded, marvelled at his conversational tone and with tremendous effort managed to find a voice that sounded reasonably controlled. 'Y-yes.' She hesitated. She had found out only this afternoon, had deliberately not allowed herself to think about it, but now here was her chance. She didn't want to interview him. She just couldn't. But explaining that to the producers, to Lizzie, to anyone, was virtually impossible—she had agreed before; they wouldn't understand why she couldn't do it again. 'Drew...' She faltered; strain etched her profile, altered the tone of her voice. Her fingers fluttered nervously to her hair and she smoothed back some loose strands from the sleek chignon at the nape of her neck. Oh, God how she hated the prospect of asking him a favour of any sort.

'Yes?' His eyes were cool and unhelpful as he turned towards her.

Surely, she thought, surely he knows what I'm about to say. Surely he can see that it would be torture for both of us? She faltered some more, aware that if she didn't ask quickly Conrad would return and the opportunity would be lost. 'About the interview...' She paused and took another breath.

Drew cast distinctly bored eyes over her. 'What about it?'

'Well, it's not going to be particularly easy, is it? I mean,' Christy added hastily, glancing back towards the house, spotting Conrad, glancing quickly back to Drew, 'after all that's happened.'

Drew's mouth curved into a distinctly mocking smile. 'It will be intriguing,' he murmured quietly, 'if nothing else. Difficult it may be, but then we are both professionals, used to putting whatever prejudices we may hold to one side. I feel quite confident that you will succeed in presenting a balanced, fair view——'

Drew, please! I don't want to do it! The words screamed silently in her head. Christy pressed her lips together to stop them escaping. He knew exactly what she wanted and yet he was determined to make her suffer some more. She wouldn't give him the satisfaction of hearing her beg. She wouldn't!

It was too late anyway. Conrad was approaching. With hands shaking perceptibly Christy managed a warm smile at Conrad and took the long, cool glass from him. 'I'll just drink this and then we'll go,' she murmured softly, adding as an afterthought, because she didn't want to give Drew any further impressions that all she had to do as far as Conrad was concerned was whistle, 'If that's all right with you, of course. We can go back to my place if you like. I'll...I'll cook us something to eat.'

'Really?' Conrad sounded as astonished as he looked.

Christy blushed and nodded, realising she had gone a little over the top because Drew was within earshot, because in some pathetic way it would annoy him to have her extend this invitation to Conrad alone. I'm being so childish, she thought. Do I really believe making him jealous will achieve anything?

'Would you like to join us, Drew?'

Christy felt herself grow pale. She jerked alarmed eyes to Conrad's face and saw that his expression showed hope as he extended the invitation to Drew.

Please no! she thought frantically. Don't do this to me. 'I'm afraid the invitation only extended to you, Conrad,' Christy cut in quickly, 'I haven't enough food in the house, and besides, my culinary efforts aren't fit for public consumption.'

'I'm public?' Drew murmured quietly, incredulously, spearing Christy with an expression that made her want to shake.

'No, of course you're not! You must come!' Conrad cut in cheerfully, oblivious of the tension that sparked all around him. He placed a reassuring arm around Christy's shoulders and it was all she could do not to shrug it off, so angry was she with him for wanting Drew to be there. 'It's a well-known fact that Christy can't cook for toffee, but we humour her and encourage her and then we go out and get some take-away.'

'I see.' Drew's mouth curled. 'Well, in that case, why not? You have no objections, Christy?' He watched and waited, which was more than Conrad did.

'Of course Christy doesn't mind!' he interposed jovially. 'It would be an honour for us both. I'm a great admirer of your work, Drew...'

No! This couldn't be happening! Christy stared wildly at Drew, saw the predatory gleam in his eyes as Conrad chattered on. How could he do this to her? She wouldn't have it! She wouldn't let him take control all over again! No! No!

'No...!' As the sound of the negative cry whispered faintly into the warm night air, Christy fell to the floor and fainted into blessed oblivion.

CHAPTER TEN

WHEN she came to, Christy found herself being driven through the darkened London streets at speed. It took a moment for her senses to come to terms with the fact that she was inside Drew's Ferrari, that he was at the wheel driving with serious intent through the relatively quiet back-streets of London.

'Would ... would you mind telling me what's happened? Why I'm in this car with you?' Her voice was shaky; she still couldn't quite organise her thoughts into any coherent pattern.

'You fainted.' Drew glanced across at her, his stunning eyes surveying her pale face for a moment. 'At the party. Don't you remember?'

Christy took a deep breath and nodded distractedly. 'Yes,' she murmured. 'Yes, I remember ...' She waited, steadying herself with her hand placed over her mouth and wished she didn't feel quite so unusually nauseous. 'You haven't,' she added, taking a great gulp of the evening air that was blowing refreshingly through the open car window, 'answered my other question. Why am I in this car with you? And where's Conrad; he was with me, wasn't he?' Suddenly she wasn't quite sure. She rubbed at her forehead and tried to think straight. It was difficult. With Drew beside her... Christy closed her eyes again and released a controlled breath. She had thought of practically little else except Drew and the two of them together. Her life had felt as if it was on hold for the last four weeks, waiting, all the time waiting...

'He's probably running around like a demented hen looking for you,' Drew continued, a spark of amusement lighting his features. 'He's not a great one for a crisis, is he?'

'What do you mean?' Christy sat more upright and forced herself to focus on Drew's words, to think about Conrad.

'Oh, he was flapping about, fussing over you. I told him to go inside and phone for a doctor and while he was in there I picked you up and carried you to my car.'

'You did what?' Christy's expression revealed her incredulity. 'You mean Conrad doesn't even know where I am?' she demanded.

'Now don't start getting yourself all worked up!' Drew commanded with the most amazing cool, considering, Christy thought, he had just performed what amounted to an act of virtual kidnap. 'I saw Monica, the host, and mentioned you'd fainted; she'll tell Conrad that you're being very well looked after.'

'I can't believe you've done this!' Christy responded in amazement, shaking her head a little, turning her face towards the open passenger window, allowing the night air to cool her hot head. 'I went to that party with Conrad, not you!' She turned back and speared him with a look of sheer incredulity, her eyes narrowed with pure anger. 'You don't give a damn, do you?'

'For Conrad, do you mean?' He turned at her question and she saw the uncaring, dismissive shrug. 'No, I don't. The man's a fool! What on earth do you see in him? He puts me in mind of an old woman!'

'Do you have to be so obnoxious?' Christy hissed through clenched teeth. 'Besides, I'll be an old woman one day, so——'

'Ah, but you'll have grace and style!' Drew cut in crisply. 'You'll possess fight and spirit. Conrad wouldn't know any of those attributes if they got up and hit him in the face!'

'You're a real pig, do you know that?' Christy snapped. 'How dare you come charging back into my life, interfering, treating me as if I'm one of your possessions or something?'

'Don't try and pretend that you prefer Conrad's company to mine,' Drew replied carelessly. 'It doesn't take an idiot to see that you're not the least bit interested in him as a man, as a lover.'

'So what makes you an expert all of a sudden?' Christy flashed. 'How do you know what goes on, what *has* gone on, between Conrad and myself? You've been away for over a month; our relationship might have progressed——'

'So have you slept with him, then, is that what you're saying?' His voice suddenly held a steel edge, suddenly sounded cold and savage.

'That's . . . that's got nothing to do with you!' Her voice wobbled alarmingly. 'What goes on between Conrad and myself is . . . is . . .'

Drew slowed the Ferrari and manoeuvred it into a space. 'Do you love him?' he asked, turning to face Christy as he switched off the engine. 'Is that what all this evasion is about? Have I read the situation wrongly?'

'Do you always have to be so sickeningly direct?' Christy countered, playing for time, because of course she knew the answer, but she wasn't sure yet if she wished Drew to know it.

'Well?' His eyes never left her face.

'I don't see what that question has to do with you!' she replied breezily, disconcerted by his intent expression. 'I'd be extremely grateful if you'd mind your own business!'

'You make it sound as if I'm just a passing stranger,' Drew grated in disbelief. 'Has fainting displaced your memory, perhaps? Have you forgotten the fact that we have been as intimate with one another as any man and woman on this earth?' His eyes flared and he leant towards her, swiftly lowering his head until his lips grazed her mouth in a ruthless, erotic kiss that took Christy totally by surprise and left her trembling with weakness and desire. 'You remember now?' Drew raised his head and slanted her a taunting look. 'Yes, I see you do! Good.'

'You haven't got a decent bone in your body, have you?' Christy murmured shakily.

'Now, Christy, there's precious little point in fobbing me off. You know, I think, that I'm the sort of man who expects an answer to my questions,' Drew replied, lifting a hand to gently ease away a strand of golden hair from her face, managing somehow, with just the lightest, most innocuous of touches, to set her heart racing all over again. 'Tell me. I think it would be a good idea if I knew exactly how things stood. After all, I wouldn't want to get the wrong idea.' He raised a dark, quizzical brow. 'Perhaps the two of you do indulge in some sort of lifeless relationship. So?'

Christy released a short, tense breath and then shook her head. 'No,' she murmured quietly, 'we don't. Satisfied?' She stared down at her own fingers, which were entwined in her lap. 'I don't love him.'

'And me?'

'What?' Her voice was barely a whisper as she found her eyes being drawn by his gaze, the depth of his voice. Was he asking her if she loved him?

'Do you really hate me so very much?'

Hate him! She should, if her head had any say in the matter, she really should. Or dislike him at the very least. But somehow intellect and practical common sense had been totally defeated by an emotion that was far more powerful. She knew exactly how she *should* feel for Drew, exactly what reply she *should* give. Hadn't he made her life a misery? Hadn't he done his level best to humiliate her?

Christy hesitated for a long moment as her mind raced over their shared history, and then, with her heart beating wildly, she lied, hoping that somehow it would cure her of this maddening, all-consuming feeling. 'Y-yes I . . . I do.'

He was unperturbed by her hesitant response. She saw the twist of a smile at the corners of his mouth, knew that she had lied for nothing, because he didn't believe a word of it.

'Do you always lie so unconvincingly, Christy?' He shook his head tauntingly, immediately creating the old spark of angry tension in the confines of the car. 'Well, at least it's a positive response, I suppose,' he drawled; 'at least I incite something other than apathy, which is more than can be said for poor old Conrad.'

Christy lifted her head. 'I like him,' she replied stubbornly. 'He's a good friend.'

'"Like" doesn't interest me, Christy. Neither does the phrase "just good friends"; you should know that by now.' He got out and strolled around the car to open the passenger door. 'Well, come on inside; my latest residence awaits your inspection.'

'I want to go home.'

'Now don't start being petulant. I'll take you later.' He held out his hand. 'Come on; you can have a brandy and then we can talk.'

Christy stared at the outstretched hand, glanced up at the dark, powerful figure of Drew, illuminated faintly by the light from a distant street-lamp, and told herself that if she fell for this she would fall for anything. What would they talk about? The weather? Politics? The dreadful state of the world's environment? Trivial things like that or something big, something that mattered, something that Christy had been fighting to come to terms with ever since that moment by the loch? She had known since then that she loved him, but she had kept it a secret even from herself. To acknowledge that the turmoil of emotion, the agony of wanting him so much was love would be like admitting defeat. How could Christy King love Drew Michaels? How could she?

He reached forward then and his fingers tightened around her hand and in the next moment she was allowing Drew to lead her up the short flight of steps to the house.

'The designers have just finished. I wanted it elegant but sort of simple. Tell me what you think.' He flicked a light switch once they were both inside and Christy saw polished wood and pale walls and pictures and books.

'It's . . .' She swallowed and tried to focus her mind on something normal. 'Y-yes . . .' She feigned interest, glancing around, seeing nothing, aware only of Drew close beside her, the brush of his arm against her body, his overwhelming physical presence... Christy cleared her throat. 'It is ... very nice——'

She felt the tug then of his hand and suddenly she was close against him and all she could see, all she could feel and touch was Drew.

'Forget the decoration,' he growled, 'forget all the small talk. We both know what we want.' He pushed her back against the wall and ran his hands lightly across her breasts, down the length of her thighs, felt the shiver of desire that swamped Christy's whole being, and did it again and again, looking into her eyes all the while, watching, a satisfied smile curving his lips as he heard a gasp escape from her lips. 'These past four weeks have been a nightmare,' he groaned. 'Wanting you in Australia, remembering the way it was ... Hell, Christy! Are you aware of what you do to me?' His mouth grazed her lips, his hands roamed almost wildly through the long silken strands of her hair. 'You must know that I want you. You must feel this tension that vibrates around us whenever we're in the same room together.' He held her chin with one strong hand and kissed her with a lazy dominance that was wholly erotic. 'Tell me I'm not imagining it, Christy. Admit that you feel it too.'

She wanted to. Oh, how much. She wanted to wrap her arms around his neck and hold him tight and tell him that she had never experienced such intense feelings before, never.

I love you. She spoke the words in her head and knew that they sounded good; that they were the truth and she could deny them no longer. He had said that he wanted her. It had been an urgent statement—a sexually hungry one, and it had sent a thrill of desire through every part of her. So he hadn't spoken those magic few words, so there was unlikely to be any long-term commitment—the alternative—that was unthinkable, unbearable. These past four weeks had shown her that.

Christy lifted her arms, placed them on his broad shoulders and with a deep, steadying breath prepared to utter the words that would commit her to Drew for better or worse. She had spent too long fighting the inevitable...

'Drew? I thought I heard the...the door.' The voice, sounding startled undoubtedly because of the scene it was witnessing, came from somewhere behind them—a shy, hesitant voice that sounded as if it belonged to a little girl.

Drew turned sharply, and Christy felt dread run through her. His reaction had been immediate. This girl was important, she meant something to him, it mattered that she was here, now, witnessing this scene that Christy had waited four weeks for.

She closed her eyes and prayed swiftly in that moment, prayed that the figure would be a female who hadn't yet reached puberty. Perhaps the daughter of a friend, a young niece perhaps? Anybody, but please, God, she thought desperately, not a woman—not *Drew's* woman!

Her face was instantly recognisable. The scene in the restaurant, gone over so many times in Christy's head, flew back to her. His companion that night when she had made a scene over the table.

Christy's violet eyes took in the attractive round face, the mass of curly auburn hair, noting with detached calm that she was a stylish dresser, very well-groomed, not a bit like an adolescent teenager. Oh, yes, and there was that little something extra to distinguish her from the rest of the crowd: this woman had one arm in plaster and she was also heavily pregnant.

'Annette! Are you OK?' Drew's voice was deep, showing immense concern. Christy stood transfixed as he dropped his arms from around her shoulders and hurried over to the bottom tread of the stairs.

She did look pale; there was a mixture of bemusement and shock written clearly over her face— like a mirror image of my own expression, Christy thought helplessly.

'Hey! Steady now. Don't cry. Shh. Shh.'

It was the most heart-rending thing to hear Drew murmur words in that deep, magnetic voice, to watch as he hugged his woman close, stroked her hair back from her tear-streaked face, holding her gently in his arms.

She should be bawling him out, Christy thought. She should be screaming at him, hitting him, not crying like a baby, accepting what she had just seen.

But then, there was the fundamental reason why Drew would always be the wrong man for her, she acknowledged with desolation. She could never accept his little ways, come to terms with the fact that clearly one woman wasn't enough.

Annette was desperately upset and he was having a difficult time calming her. Christy gave them one last glance and then, turning silently, opened the front door and disappeared out into the night.

She walked for hours, finally ending up in an all-night café, incongruously dressed in her long, swirling skirt of flame and gold, with her hair tousled and her face pale, going over and over all that had happened, trying to adjust to the fact that all her hopes had been destroyed.

Lizzie looked quite shocked when Christy arrived for breakfast, even more shocked when, after a halting explanation, she burst into tears on the doorstep and sobbed herself dry on the cluttered, sagging settee.

'I just had no idea!' Lizzie kept saying. 'You always disliked Drew so much—let's be honest, hated him. And now——'

'I *do* hate him!' Christy's voice revealed all her hurt and pain as her eyes flashed with anger. 'I do! And more than that I hate myself too. For being so naïve, for hoping and believing in such stupid notions, such ridiculous fantasies. She was pregnant, Lizzie. And so distraught. I felt quite sorry for her, even though it was killing me to watch as he held her and spoke to her...' She shook her head violently, annoyed by the tears which insisted on falling again, angered by how easily her mind replayed the scenes that hurt the most. 'He's always kept his private life totally secret, hasn't he? Oh, I knew there had been women—lots of them. But fool that I am...well, I just imagined...I mean, I couldn't believe...'

'But if she's pregnant, Christy...' Lizzie murmured quietly. 'You said several months—well, it isn't easy, is it? Perhaps he would have liked to break with her, but if she's carrying his child he does have certain commitments, doesn't he? Oh, sorry, Christy!' Lizzie put her arm around her friend's shoulders, hugging her tight. 'I didn't mean to make you feel any worse——'

Christy closed her eyes in anguish. Carrying Drew's child! She pictured Annette, blooming despite her

pallor and the broken arm. What must it feel like—
Drew's own seed creating new life inside you?

'Don't...don't worry, Lizzie.' She forced air into
her lungs and stood up, wrapping her arms tight
around her body. 'I couldn't feel much worse anyway.'
She managed a watery smile. 'Thanks for being here...
I had to see someone... I've been going over and
over everything all night.' She gulped a breath. 'Could
you call a taxi for me? I need to go home now, get
some sleep.'

'Of course.' Lizzie picked up the phone immediately. 'What will you do—tomorrow, the next day?
Will you see him?'

'Oh, no!' Christy spun away and gazed out of the
window at the busy streets below. 'I'm going to take
some time off. To hell with my commitments for this
new series. They can postpone or get someone else
in—if I were ill that's what would happen anyway.'
And God knows I feel bad enough, she thought as
tears misted her eyes once again. She sniffed and
rubbed a tissue over her eyes. 'I think I'll take a few
weeks' holiday. Some place where I can rest and
forget. Some distant, exotic island where no one's even
heard of Drew Michaels!'

'Is there such a place?' Lizzie asked seriously.

Christy shrugged hopelessly and managed a watery
smile. 'If there isn't, Lizzie,' she whispered chok-
ingly, 'I think I'll go mad.'

CHAPTER ELEVEN

CHRISTY pushed open her front door and dropped her gold evening bag down on to the hall table. She felt like death warmed up. Chilled and tired and hungry and totally, totally miserable.

She leant back against the wall and looked around her. This house was her pride and joy. It encompassed her whole self. Every room full of elaborate furnishings and expensive artifacts. It was solid, undeniable proof that she, Christy King, had succeeded where others had failed.

Succeeded? Christy shook her head slowly and moved through the rooms, fingering items as she went. Such a lot of money, such a lot of work—and for what? She was alone. This place was a shell where she came and went, no more than that. Perhaps it would be good to get away for a while. She needed to think things out; she needed to reassess her life. Decide where she went from here.

She released a small breath of anguish and curled her fingers around a small bronze statue, gripping the cold metal hard until she felt the rough lines of the sculpture's work hurting her skin. She had found the one man that meant more than anything to her, experienced for brief moments the meaning of true fulfilment, and discovered that where there should have been lasting joy only misery and heartache reigned.

'You shouldn't have left like that.'

Christy felt sure that her heart would stop, so violent was its beating. She looked down at the statue unblinkingly, then she turned very slowly and directed her gaze in the direction of Drew's voice.

He looked magnificent. Dark and brooding, wearing that special aura that was his alone around him like an impenetrable cloak. Her eyes registered his presence, told her that he really was lounging comfortably on a sofa in her drawing-room with his long, muscular legs stretched out before him and his handsome head resting against the plush upholstered cushion, but her brain struggled to accept the reality.

She gulped oxygen into her lungs and moved forward with slow, hesitant steps, gripping the back of a nearby chair for support.

'Where have you been?' His voice was calm, conversational, almost as if she had, Christy thought, just popped out on an unexpected errand. But underneath the smooth, unruffled surface wasn't there just the slightest edge, the latent sign of unmistakable anger?

She tried to swallow, but her mouth was dry. There was a wild beating in her head that made thinking, moving, even feeling difficult. 'H-how did you get in?' It was a mundane question, totally irrelevant considering the million and one things Christy wanted to know, or rather didn't want to know, but it was at least a start.

'Your neighbour—Mrs McCarthy, is it?'

'McCormack,' Christy corrected automatically.

'Yes, of course. Well, I spun her a yarn about a mix-up over the keys and she was only too pleased to oblige. An admirer, you see.' Drew's mouth curved attractively. 'They're very easy to win over.'

'Con, don't you mean?' Christy's voice was taut, her face felt as stiff as a board, her whole body rigid with the effort of keeping her emotions in check. How could he just walk in like this, sit there, talk so calmly, when she had gone through agonies all night just going over and over the fact that he didn't really give a damn about her?

'You haven't slept?' His steely blue eyes ran over Christy's dishevelled outfit from the evening before in slow appraisal and then came back to rest on her pale face. 'Where did you go?'

'That's...that's my business!' She gulped a breath. Better, Christy! she told herself. Much better! Keep it up. Hang on to your pride. Don't let him see what an emotional wreck he's turned you into.

She moved over to the window and drew back the curtains a little wider so that rays of cheerful morning sunshine streamed into the room. 'Now if you don't mind——!'

'I think perhaps we'd better talk, but after you've had a bath and slept,' Drew responded coolly. 'I had hoped that we could get this misunderstanding sorted out quickly, but I can see that you're in no fit state to listen or think clearly now. You'll feel better after——'

'Don't order me about in my own home!' Christy gritted through clenched teeth. 'Don't you dare! I don't want to talk to you—isn't that fact as clear as crystal? I don't want you here patronising me with your casual demeanour, talking to me as if I'm a child!' She shook her head and threw him a look of utter fury. 'Misunderstanding? What a very convenient way of describing your deceit and your lies——'

'Christy——!'

'Don't Christy me! Don't even talk to me!' she flared wildly, ignoring Drew's warning tones. 'Just get out. Leave me alone. Stop making my life an absolute misery!' She spun away from him, pressing trembling fingers against her lips as she felt physical sickness rising, the weird light-headed sensation in her head that she had experienced on and off over the last few days.

'You have to know about Annette.'

'No! No!' Christy frantically clapped her hands over her ears. 'I've seen all I need to see. I don't want to hear about her. I don't want to hear all the usual phrases, listen to the deceit and the lies!' She turned away from him and looked out through the window at the tree-lined street. 'You used me, Drew, and I allowed it to happen. Can't you understand how that makes me feel?'

'No, I cannot! Because none of it's true.' She heard movement from behind her and then the sound of Drew's feet on the polished wooden floor. 'Deceit? Lies? What lies? What deception? When? Where?' His voice was harsh now, possessing as much, if not more fury than Christy's. She felt his hand on her arm and she gasped audibly as he dragged her unceremoniously round to face him.

He looked more wild than she had ever seen him before; his eyes glinted fire. She stood shaking before him, her breathing coming in ragged, convulsive gulps. When he was as close as this it was so hard to continue with the anger and the hate despite everything...

She felt faint again. The shock of seeing him like this when she was at her most vulnerable was obviously doing her no good at all. She raised her free hand and pressed it against her forehead, aware that quite suddenly she felt so weird, so weak and light-headed. Hold on, she told herself. Take deep breaths; you can't keel over at Drew's feet now, not again . . .

But she did.

She felt herself being lifted, was aware of the pleasant shock of cool sheets and then she was opening her eyes and looking into Drew's incredibly handsome face. She smiled and felt a delicious feeling of pleasure run through her body, because he was near, taking care of her. She lifted a hand and brought it up to his face, lightly tracing the furrowed brow and the taut, angular jaw with its new dark growth, enjoying the rough feel of his unshaven skin beneath the smooth tips of her fingers.

'You fainted again, Christy.' His voice sounded just wonderful too—deep and husky, thick with an emotion that she couldn't quite understand. 'I've sent for your doctor.'

But something was wrong. What was it? Christy narrowed her gaze, forced herself to focus properly and realised that his expression was an unusual one. She inhaled deeply and struggled to sit up, remembering in that same moment that things weren't right between them, recalling with agonising clarity the scene that had taken place between them minutes— or was it hours?—before.

'I don't need a doctor.' She withdrew her hand sharply and gripped the bedclothes instead, noting that her arms were bare, that Drew must have re-moved the crumpled skirt and top. She slid further down beneath the counterpane, aware that her lacy bra was revealing in the extreme. 'It's because I haven't eaten, haven't slept ... Look, please go and call him back, say you made a mistake. I'm all right!'

'No, I will not!' Drew informed her steadily. 'You look deathly pale and this is the second time you've fainted in my arms. Once is wonderful, twice makes me uneasy—you know as well as I do, Christy, that you're not the fainting type.' He turned his head towards the elegantly festooned bedroom window. 'That sounds like a car pulling up outside now. It will probably be him.'

He rose from the bed and left the room and Christy listened anxiously to the sound of the front door and muffled voices and then steeled herself for the unnecessary appearance of the doctor who would surely rebuke them both for wasting his time.

'You are pregnant, my dear.'

Christy stared up into the kindly, well-worn face and knew that what the doctor was saying was the truth. He had asked her if it was a possibility and she had, after a moment's shocked, unbelieving silence, nodded dumbly. Now, after a visit to the bathroom, after a quick test that had taken no more than a couple of seconds, Christy knew the reason for her fainting attacks, her bouts of nausea.

She was carrying Drew's child.

Why, oh, why hadn't it occurred to her before? All the obvious signs had been there—or rather had not been there—but she had simply put it down to stress, over-work. Anything, everything, except the most sensible and logical explanation.

Her mind swung back to the moment beside the loch. It had been the most wonderful experience of her life—a night to remember. She had conceived this

baby there. Christy closed her eyes and remembered
the glorious feeling as Drew had taken absolute pos-
session of her...

'Miss King?' She looked up and realised with embarrassment that the doctor had been standing beside
the bed looking down at her for some length of time.
He smiled knowingly. 'A shock,' he murmured, 'but
evidently not an unwelcome one.'

Christy released a breath and felt the colour
flooding her face. Was it unwelcome? How should
she feel? Good, bad, indifferent? No, not that.
Indifferent to carrying her own and Drew Michaels'
child? Never.

She was having trouble with her concentration.
Christy tried to focus her thoughts.

'So I suggest you rest for a few days,' the doctor
was saying. 'I'll prescribe you some iron tablets. They
will certainly help with the tiredness you have been
experiencing.'

'Dr Marshall!' Christy was aware of the anxious
tone of her own voice, felt the panic rising steadily
within her. He turned at the door and raised enquiring brows. 'You...you won't mention this to
anyone...I mean, when you go downstairs——'

'Mr Michaels, do you mean?' The doctor shook his
head and gave a little frown. 'Of course not, my dear.
There is such a thing as medical ethics. Now don't
look so worried; try and get some rest.'

Don't worry? Christy laid her head back against
the pillow and closed her eyes in despair after the
doctor had left the room. What was she going to do?

'Can I come in?' Drew had silently opened the door
and was poised on the threshold. He moved towards
the bed without a word and stood gazing down at her.

'You've been overdoing it, I gather. Complete rest, the doctor said, for a couple of days at least. What's this?' His long brown fingers picked up the prescription that had been left on the bedside table.

'Oh, it's...it's for some iron tablets,' Christy breathed. 'I'm a bit anaemic.'

Deep blue eyes surveyed her rigid expression. 'Are you sure you're all right?' he asked quietly.

'Yes!' Her voice rose an octave. 'Please, Drew, go. I'm just tired. I need some sleep——'

'I'm not leaving.' His voice, his eyes bit into her. 'I'll go down to the chemist and get this prescription seen to. And then after you're rested we'll talk—or at least I'm going to talk; you need to listen.'

It was early afternoon when Christy awoke. She had amazed herself by falling into a deep sleep the moment Drew had left. It had been an enjoyable few hours. In her dreams life had been good again and she had been with Drew and so of course she had been happy...

She screwed her eyes shut and swallowed back the lump in her throat. Pregnant. What a foolish, foolish thing to allow to happen. Two women carrying Drew's child...

So what should she do? Terminate this life inside her? It was still early; there was still plenty of time in which to have an abortion. Instinctively her hand slid over the still flat plane of her stomach. No. That wasn't for her. Killing a part of her and a part of Drew just couldn't be contemplated.

Keep it, then. But to tell Drew... The feeling of panic returned. How could she find the strength to do that? What would it achieve?

I'm so confused, she thought hopelessly. I love him so much and I want his baby, but if I tell him about it... So what *would* happen? She tried to imagine, tried to picture any amount of different reactions...

'Good, you're awake.' Drew came in carrying a tray on which was a tasty selection of morsels that Christy knew hadn't come from her kitchen. She eyed the selection of cold meats and various delicious-looking salads and realised that despite everything she was incredibly hungry.

'You went out for these?' Her voice was quiet, a little unsteady.

'Sure did.' Drew gave her face a searching look and then set the tray across her lap. 'You should have seen the commotion. The shopkeeper's eyes were as round and large as plates.'

'Were there lots of people?'

'Quite a few—or at least it seemed that way.'

'Were they aggressive?' Christy pictured various incidents that she had witnessed outside the television centre—she knew only too well that everything could get out of hand so quickly. 'I mean——'

Drew's mouth curved. 'You mean am I hurt? No, it was all very good-natured. Everyone got an autograph and for once that seemed to satisfy them.'

'Have...have you ever been mobbed really badly?' Christy found herself asking, aware that the thought of Drew being injured in any way filled her with an overriding sense of concern.

'Oh, I've come close a couple of times,' he replied casually. 'But then I'm a stubborn son of a bitch and I absolutely refuse to give up my liberty whatever the price.' He paused and touched Christy's hair. 'That's why I'm here now.'

Christy raised large violet eyes to his face. 'W-what do you mean?'

'I'm stubborn,' Drew repeated softly. 'I don't give in easily. Surely you've realised that much about me. When I want something—someone——'

'Drew, please!' Christy turned her head on the pillow, felt the sting of tears hurting her eyes. 'I . . . I really can't handle this right now——'

'I'm not going anywhere until we get this thing straightened out, Christy,' he told her adamantly, gently easing her face back around to his. 'You've jumped to a million wrong conclusions. You've made yourself as miserable as hell and all for nothing.' He paused and placed a light finger on her lips to prevent her from speaking. 'Annette's not my woman, Christy, and she's not carrying my child.'

'What?' Her voice was the barest whisper.

'It's the truth,' Drew murmured softly. 'I would never lie to you about something as important as that.'

'But. . . but the two of you . . . she was at your house . . . and with you before in the restaurant, and when she began crying I——'

'You jumped to the wrong conclusion.'

'I did?'

'We've been friends for a long while, Christy—platonic friends, nothing more. You see, she was once married to my brother. They split up a few years ago, but we've stayed in contact. I like her, she's a genuine, caring person, but that really is as far as it goes.' He waited a moment, allowing Christy a chance to query what he said, disbelieve him. When she made no reply he continued. 'Recently she found herself in a situation that she just couldn't handle. My brother lives abroad permanently now, so she came to me.'

'Oh, I . . . I see.'

'Do you?' Drew asked her seriously, his dark brows raised in query.

No, Christy thought, I don't think I do. 'Did you go to see her that night when you left the farmhouse?'

'Yes.'

'You drove all the way to London? But why?' Her voice rose with agitation. 'It's such a long way and we were . . . I mean, everything was going so well.' She gazed at him and added mournfully, 'I just don't understand.'

'Believe me, if it hadn't have been so urgent I wouldn't have left. I considered taking you with me, but I honestly thought it would be far better if you stayed at the farmhouse and waited for me to return. Hospitals and police stations aren't the sort of places——'

'Hospital?' Christy shook her head in confusion. 'Drew, you haven't explained properly—what about hospitals and police stations? What on earth have they got to do with anything?'

'Haven't I?' He gave a rueful shake of his head and suddenly she saw that he looked a little unlike his usual self, sort of different, just a little confused. 'No, I haven't, have I? Sorry, sweetheart.' He touched her cheek very softly and it was all Christy could do not to swoon back into a faint all over again. He had called her sweetheart. It was the very first endearment he had used. Sweetheart.

'Annette's lover beats her,' Drew informed her. 'This so-called boyfriend finds it perfectly reasonable behaviour to lash out at her now and then, particularly when he's been drinking. Apparently he wasn't too pleased at discovering she was pregnant and things have gradually got worse ever since. Anyway, she really had no one else to turn to, no one at least who could deal with this sort of situation, so I've been helping her, giving her a refuge while she tried to sort her life out.'

'He broke her arm?' Christy's expression conveyed her horror.

Drew nodded grimly. 'That plus a few other delightful little bruises in places that aren't quite so noticeable. The culprit's finally been tracked down now and is in custody, and Annette, I'm glad to say, has come to her senses at last and gone back to stay with her widowed mother in the north.' He shook his head in bewilderment. 'How she could ever have kidded herself that she loved the bastard is quite beyond me,' he added savagely.

'No, I know what you mean—but then love is a funny thing,' Christy whispered; 'it turns you inside out, upside-down ...' She bit down on her bottom lip and struggled against the tears that were filling her eyes.

'Yes.' Drew's voice was husky suddenly. 'It's taken me completely by surprise.' He bent over her and kissed the tears that had spilled over on to her cheeks. 'Three years, Christy—it's a long time. Do you know you would come into my mind in the most unexpected moments? Ridiculous, I thought, and I fought it every step of the way, but in the end even I, strong-willed, stubborn son of a bitch Drew Michaels, couldn't cope with my life as it was any more.' He raised his head and she saw the smouldering look in his eyes. 'I need you. I love you, Christy, utterly, absolutely, without any shadow of a doubt.' His mouth curved into a stunning smile. 'You must know that surely?'

A rush of extreme happiness, unlike anything she had ever experienced before, surged through her as Drew bent and sealed his words of love with a kiss that was pure commitment, pure sincerity, pure desire. He loved her! Christy could hardly believe it. He really and truly loved her!

But what about the baby? Like a cloud it loomed on the horizon, threatening to spoil the moment. Would it be grey and black as night, threatening a storm of disapproval, rejection, indifference, or would it be the light cirrus variety that formed at high altitude and heralded blue skies and brilliant sun? Christy held her breath and prayed silently. Please, God, don't let it change things . . .

With great reluctance she eased his body back from hers. She wanted to hold him fiercely, tenderly, to allow the hands that were roaming her body free rein; but first, first she had to tell him about the baby.

'Drew, there's something you need to know—two things.' He raised his head and she saw him frown slightly at the seriousness of her tone. 'First of all . . .' she paused fractionally, gazing up at him with eyes that conveyed all of her emotions ' . . . I love you. I love you very much.' She caught her breath, felt a *frisson* of desire race through her as Drew's smouldering eyes consumed every part of her and his hand reached out and touched her face. 'Secondly . . .' She hesitated. 'Secondly . . .' Tell him, she thought; do it now, before you lose the courage. 'I . . . I'm pregnant. I'm carrying your child.' Her words had finished in a rush. She stared up at him, feeling very much a woman, but also like a little girl who had

owned up to some deed and was not sure of the reaction or the outcome of her honesty.

Drew looked at her for a long moment and then
slowly he lowered his head and Christy knew as he
buried his face in her shoulder that everything was
going to be all right—no, better than all right—simply
wonderful, simply perfect.

'My darling,' he whispered tenderly. 'Oh, my
beautiful, beautiful darling.'

He touched her then. Gently, searchingly, almost
reverently, each hand tracing a symmetrical path down
the line of her throat, along the edges of her bare
shoulders, over the thin straps, along the pale golden
arms, then across to her body, lightly over the lacy
fabric that covered her breasts, pushing back the bedclothes, smoothing the flat plane of her stomach...on
and on...further down until Christy felt weak, faint
again, but this time with desire and need.

'Christy...' He raised his eyes to her face and they
conveyed everything she needed to know; such a look
of love, such depth and passion.

She raised a hand and pressed one finger softly
against Drew's lips. 'Don't say anything,' she whispered. 'Just show me...'

And he did.

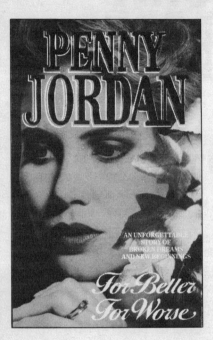

Next Month's Romances

Each month you can choose from a wide variety of romance with Mills & Boon. Below are the new titles to look out for next month, why not ask either Mills & Boon Reader Service or your Newsagent to reserve you a copy of the titles you want to buy – just tick the titles you would like and either post to Reader Service or take it to any Newsagent and ask them to order your books.

Please save me the following titles:		Please tick	✓
A MASTERFUL MAN	Lindsay Armstrong		
WAITING GAME	Diana Hamilton		
DARK FATE	Charlotte Lamb		
DEAREST MARY JANE	Betty Neels		
WEB OF DARKNESS	Helen Brooks		
DARK APOLLO	Sara Craven		
BLUE FIRE	Sarah Holland		
MASTER OF EL CORAZON	Sandra Marton		
A WAYWARD LOVE	Emma Richmond		
TANGLED DESTINIES	Sara Wood		
THE RIGHT KIND OF MAN	Jessica Hart		
DANGEROUS ENTANGLEMENT	Susanne McCarthy		
THE HEAT OF THE MOMENT	Kay Gregory		
AN EASY MAN TO LOVE	Lee Stafford		
THE BEST-MADE PLANS	Leigh Michaels		
NEW LEASE ON LOVE	Shannon Waverly		

If you would like to order these books in addition to your regular subscription from Mills & Boon Reader Service please send £1.90 per title to: Mills & Boon Reader Service, Freepost, P.O. Box 236, Croydon, Surrey, CR9 9EL, quote your Subscriber No:.................... (if applicable) and complete the name and address details below. Alternatively, these books are available from many local Newsagents including W H Smith, J Menzies, Martins and other paperback stockists from 14 October 1994.

Name:..

Address:..

....Post Code:..........................

To Retailer: If you would like to stock M&B books please contact your regular book/magazine wholesaler for details.